RAGE'S REDEMPTION

Wild Kings MC

Rage's Redemption
By: Erin Osborne

Copyright

Cover Design: Graphics by Shelly

Editor: Jenni Copeland Belanger

Dedication

This book is dedicated to the readers. Without you, none of us would be able to live our dream and do something that we love to do. You have stood by my side and shown me more support than I ever dreamed possible. Thank you from the bottom of my heart!!

Table Of Contents

Prologue

Keegan

THE FIRST NIGHT THAT RAGE and Kasey stayed for dinner was an event that changed everything. Or maybe it was just the kiss that changed everything. I'm not sure what it was, but things definitely changed in that moment. Rage has been here almost daily on top of when he's guarding the house. I'm not sure exactly why they're guarding the house, but there's at least three men here every day around the clock.

Before I head out today I need to check the mail. It's been a few days and, Riley, a friend from one of the towns I stayed in, was supposed to be sending me some stuff. She found a few things that I had left behind and knew I wanted them. To some it might not seem like much, but to me they're priceless. Pictures of Whitney and I when we were younger, a few that she managed to sneak out to me when Sami was younger, and three bracelets that Whit had given me shortly before she got sold. These items became my only connection to my cousin.

"Where are you headin' Keegan?" Rage asks me, standing up from his chair on the porch.

"Just to check the mail. My friend is supposed to be sending me some stuff I forgot a few months ago."

"You want me to check it for you?"

"No. Kasey is washing up before we head over to Whitney and Irish's house. I'll be right back."

The mail box is still in view considering the house doesn't sit that far from the road. I pull out the few pieces of mail I have and head back up to the house. As I'm flipping through the small stack, I see handwriting that has my blood running cold. Rage is at my side in a heartbeat, but I need to read this by myself.

"What's wrong Keegan?" he asks, trying to take the mail from me.

"Nothing. The package isn't here and it's upsetting is all," I lie. Usually I don't lie to anyone and this feels sour on my tongue. I need to know what this asshole wants before I let anyone else in on what's going on.

As soon as I'm back in the house and Rage is sitting back in his usual chair, I head into the bedroom I've been sleeping in. Sitting down on the bed, I put the rest of the mail to the side. Holding the letter, I don't want to open it, but I know I must. Even if it's just to find out what he wants and how he found me. So, I take a deep breath and then rip open the letter.

Keegan,

I don't know what you were thinking when you thought you could escape your fate. For the past sixteen years I have been trailing you all over the country. Now, I've found you in the same area as your slut of a cousin. I don't know what you are thinking, but you WILL be coming home. I owe you to Sam and you are going to him. He's been waiting a very long time for you.

So, you have three months to make your decision. That's Sam's time frame. At the end of three months, you can either make this easy or hard. If we have to come get you, you won't like what happens. This is your only warning!

Sincerely,

Your loving father

The paper falls out of my hand and lands on the floor. I was so into reading the letter that I didn't know that Rage had entered my room. Before I can react, he scoops up the letter and starts to read it. This is not what I need today. I don't need him to try to fight my battles for me and have something happen to him.

"What the fuck is this Keegan?" he asks. Even though he's yelling, I know that he's not angry with me. I can see the concern written all over his face.

"I don't want you to get involved Rage," I tell him. "This is my problem to deal with. And if you knew the things that I've had to do since I've been gone, you'd be running far away from me."

"And what do you think that you've done so wrong that would scare me away?"

"I had one person try to pimp me out. Before I could get away, he did make me go to two people. It was the worst night of my life. I've been beaten to the point that I lost my baby and then turned to drinking to forget it. When I lost my baby, I was upset, but then again, I was relieved. I didn't want my child to grow up living in a house with Sam if he ever found me. That's just a few things. I can give you a whole list of things I've had to do to survive."

"Baby, those are things that happened to you. You didn't choose to do those things. If you think that shit is goin' to scare me away, you have another thing comin'. I've learned to go after what I want and that's what I'm gonna do. You better get used to it!"

I stare at Rage in astonishment. How a man like him could want someone like me is completely beyond me. I've never seen myself as anything special. I'm just me and that's good enough for me. Rage could have anyone he wants, and I know this. I see women throwing themselves at him constantly if we go out anywhere. For the most part, he ignores them. But, that's just what I see.

And, there's the club girls that he can go to at any point in time. So, he's definitely not lacking company.

"But, what if I don't know if I'm even going to stay in Clifton Falls? I might be leaving here soon," I tell him, trying to convince myself.

"I think you know already that you're goin' to be stayin' here. There's too much here for you to want to leave. If Whitney, Sami, Cassidy, and Austin aren't enough of a reason to stay, then Kasey and I will become your reason," Rage tells me, leaning down and placing a kiss on my temple.

I can't respond to that. No matter how much I want Rage, today showed me that there can't be a relationship between us. My dad and Sam aren't ever going to leave me alone. I'm not going to bring anyone into that shit show. Kasey needs Rage around and I'm not going to risk his life for the two men looking for me. He doesn't know what they're like and what they're willing to do.

Chapter One

Rage

IT'S BEEN TWO WEEKS SINCE Keegan got the letter from her dad. We're still trying to figure out how he found her. I'm pretty sure that Whitney's dad told him where she was, but we can't prove that since we can't find him now. Irish is working extra on trying to find him since he's married to Whitney and Keegan is her cousin. He's not going to allow anything to fuck up his family.

I'm trying to stay even closer to her, but I can feel Keegan pushing me away. I know that she's scared and doesn't want anything to happen to me. What she doesn't realize is that I'm not going anywhere. We're going to explore this thing between us because I know she feels it too. And if I learned anything from what happened with Storm, it's that you go after what you want when you find it.

As usual, I'm sitting on the front porch in the chair. I'm listening to Keegan and Kasey in the house and I love hearing the laughter coming from my daughter. Unfortunately, I can't keep listening to them because there's a car coming down the road. Looking closer, I can see that it's the same car that's been here once a week since the letter arrived. Now I know what to expect. The roses.

Every week so far, Keegan gets roses dyed black and starting to wilt. They represent the number of weeks that she has left. This week, there will be ten of them. Once I realized what they were, she screamed her head off the first time she got them, I try to keep them from her sight. I don't ever want Keegan to see them again. Or the card that comes with them.

Running down the steps, I meet the delivery man before he can even get out of the car. Hell, I'm surprised he stopped with the way I met the car. Grabbing the box, I slip the card in my pocket, hand him some money, and walk towards the house. The garbage can is out front, so I throw the box right in it.

Sitting down in my usual spot, I make sure no one is looking before I pull the card out. Every week the message gets worse and I can't imagine what this one is going to say. Fuck, it's going to be bad by the time we get to the last one

Keegan,

The countdown continues. You don't seem to be taking this seriously, so I might have to persuade you. If I don't hear from you soon, someone you love will be hurt. Sam is becoming frustrated and you don't want it to get much worse.

Sincerely,

Your loving father

Keegan's dad is no loving father. What kind of man sells his daughter and then spends sixteen years chasing her? Now, he seems to be hunting her down. Too bad the chicken can't come out of hiding and show himself. I can't wait to get my hands on this fucker!

"Rage, was someone here?" Keegan asks, coming to the door.

"Um, I won't lie to you. You got another delivery. I took care of it already."

"What's the card say this time?"

"I really don't want to tell you. Or show it to you," I tell her, trying to let her see that it's not good without actually showing her.

"Rage, please?" she asks. "I need to know what is going on. If I don't know, then I won't know how to protect myself. Can you understand that?"

"I get where you're comin' from. It still doesn't make me want to tell you what it says. I'm tryin' to protect you here."

"I know you are. But, I still need to be able to protect myself. You aren't always going to be with me. And, if I'm with someone else, I need to know they're going to be okay."

Relenting, I hand the card over to her. As she's reading it, I can see the color draining from her face. She's truly scared, and not just for herself anymore. Now, she's worried about everyone around her too. As she gets to the last part of the card, I can see the decision in her eyes that she's going to run. That's not going to happen.

"You're not goin' anywhere Keegan. The safest place for you is right here. We can, and will, protect you. Don't ever doubt that," I tell her, wrapping my arm around her and making her look me directly in the eyes. Keegan needs to know I'm dead serious about protecting her.

"I have to. Can't you see that I'm bringing a world of trouble here?"

"It's not anythin' we can't handle. We took Carl down, and we'll take this asshole down too."

"You can't promise me that. You can't stand here and promise me that no one is going to get hurt," she tells me, tears shimmering in her eyes.

Keegan is trying to be so strong. She needs to learn that she can depend on us though. We will all have her back and protect her if the need arises. It's nothing that we haven't done for anyone else. There will always be someone that needs to be helped or protected, we're in a position to do that.

"I need to call Grim about this babe," I tell her. "He might want to step up the protection on you for a little bit."

"Rage, I seriously think I should leave. I won't bring them here."

"So, you'd rather go out there alone? Unprotected and alone? Are you tryin' to make sure that they get you? Do you really want to go with them? Is that what you're tryin' to get at?" I ask, my voice raising. Keegan is scared, and I know that's the reason she's pushing this issue about leaving. At this point, she's letting her fear overrule rational thought. I won't allow her to do that.

"That's not what I want!" she yells right back. "I want to live my life. There's no way I'll be able to do that there. From what I hear, Sam is worse than Carl ever thought to be."

"Okay, so why run? I know you're still gettin' to know us, but Whitney trusts us. Sami trusts us. They're your blood and they believe in us enough to let us help them. Can't you do the same?"

"It's just so hard when you've had to rely on yourself for so long. I want to believe in your club and trust you guys. I just haven't really had luck when it comes to trusting other people. Riley is the only one that's ever been true."

"Then trust in me. I've been here everyday, Keegan. We're gettin' to know one another and I want to see where this leads. Don't let them scare you away," I tell her, my voice dropping, and I feel like I'm pleading with her now.

"I'll think about it."

Keegan turns around and walks back to my daughter in the kitchen. I'll have to keep a closer eye on her to make sure that she doesn't pull a runner. There's no way that I'm letting her disappear because she can't get over her fear. I'll prove to her that we can be trusted. Even if I must play dirty and tell Whitney, Sami, and Pops what's going on. And if she won't listen to them, then I'll get Tank to work his magic. I know without a doubt they won't let her leave. And that Tank will talk her into staying. He seems to have some sort of power when it comes to talking to the women of the club.

Keegan

I truly want to believe in Rage and the Wild Kings. I've never had anyone that I could depend on, and it's been nice to have people around just to laugh and be with. Now that the cards on the flowers getting more threatening, I can't help the overwhelming feeling that I need to leave. I need to run to protect these people and make sure they don't get hurt.

For the first time in my life, I've been able to live free. I don't have to worry about someone coming after me because they want something I don't want to give. There's people that are going to have my back. Even if it's just because I'm Whitney's cousin.

Kasey has brought life back to me. She makes me laugh, smile, and be as carefree as someone can be. We spend our time baking, cooking, playing games, playing outside, and one day taking pictures. She took my phone one day and decided that she needed pictures of us, of Rage and me together, and of the three of us together. Then, we had to go to the store to get some of them printed off. Rage and I each have one of us together, Kasey made sure of it. The one I have is of him standing behind me with his arms wrapped around me.

Today Kasey is spending the day with Reagan and Skylar. So, instead of baking and cooking, I'm cleaning. The music is blaring, and the windows are wide open. Right now, *Let You Go* by *Machine Gun Kelly* is blaring throughout the house. I love the song and I have a feeling that I'm going to be telling Rage to let me go one of these days. I'm no good for him.

"What are you doin' Keegan?" Rage asks me.

"Cleaning. What are you doing?"

"Protectin' you," he answers. "And I might be watchin' you shake that fine ass."

"I don't know who you're talking about, but you might want to go chase that girl then," I tell him, turning to leave the window.

"You know exactly who I'm talkin' about Keegan," he calls out after me.

The afternoon flew by and I managed to get the entire house clean, the laundry caught up, and I spent some time with Whitney. She doesn't understand why I'm limiting my time over there, and I can't keep explaining it to her. As far as Whitney is concerned, I'm safer at her house then staying at the house with guards. I'm not going to put her and her family in danger though. Well, anymore danger than what I'm already putting them in.

I'm finally back at the house and I'm trying to figure out what I'm going to make for dinner. Tonight, I made sure that it's just going to be me. This is getting hard trying to limit the amount of time I spend with everyone. But, I'm not going to put Kasey in danger anymore either. I still watch her a little bit during the day, but I make sure that Rage and whoever else guarding me is close by at all times.

There's a knock on the door and I know that Tank is sitting out front. If whoever here wasn't safe, then they wouldn't make it past him. I'm still not taking any chances though, so I look out the door to see who it is. Standing there holding something is Rage. Kasey isn't with him tonight, so I don't know what's going on. Unless something else happened, and he's coming to warn me.

"What do you want Rage?" I ask, opening the door.

"I'm here for dinner. You're done hidin' Keegan," he tells me, walking in the house and straight to the kitchen.

"What are you talking about? I'm not hiding from anything."

"You are, and you know it. Tonight, is goin' to be about us. I'm goin' to show you what it's goin' to be like when we take it to the next level. And you can guarantee that we will be takin' it to the next level," he tells me, standing as close as possible to me.

I don't respond to him. Instead, I try to take a few steps back and put some much-needed space between us. Rage doesn't let me though. For every step I take backwards, he moves forward. Eventually, I run out of room and I find my back against the refrigerator. He uses this to his advantage and places a hand on each side of me, so I can't move anywhere. After looking at me for a minute, I see his head moving closer and closer to me. Before I know it, his lips are meeting mine in a breathtaking kiss. It's even better than the first one.

"Wow!" I say when he finally releases me.

"And you don't want to see where this is goin' to go? Come on Keegan, quit runnin' and take a chance on us."

"I want to more than you know. There's just too much going on to put you and Kasey in the middle of. I'm not going to let anything happen to that precious little angel."

"You let me worry about Kasey. She's goin' to be in our lives forever and nothin' is goin' to happen to her," he says. "Now, we're gonna eat and then I'm goin' to relax with you on the couch and we'll talk or watch movies. Today begins you not hidin' from me Keegan."

There's nothing I can say, or do, that's going to get Rage to back down. So, I move to the counter where he placed the bags and begin to remove the food he brought with him. I can already tell the food is from the Corner Café, so I know I'm going to love whatever he brought. Pulling out the containers, I see that it's cheeseburgers, fries, gravy on the side for me, and milkshakes. One of the few meals that I get when I go over there.

"Are you trying to bribe me?" I ask, knowing he pays attention to the smallest detail when I think he's not.

"Nope. I don't have to bribe you. You're goin' to realize that we're goin' to be together all on your own," Rage tells me, accepting the plate that I'm handing him.

"If you say so," I retaliate.

"I know so Keegan. I'm goin' to make it so you won't know what to do without Kasey and I in your life."

"You're already doing it," I tell him honestly.

The rest of the night sails by so smoothly. Rage is funny, smart, and so bossy at times I can't stand it. But, he's so sexy that I want nothing more than to get a piece of him. I can't concentrate on that though. That would be taking things to a new level that I don't know if I want with him. Well, I want it, I just don't know if I'm going to be able to give in to him.

"Penny for your thoughts?" he asks.

"I'm just thinking about whether or not I can take this to the next level with you. I mean, I want to, but I can't seem to bring myself to take the leap. Besides, it's only been a short time since I met you," I tell him.

"I know enough already that we're gonna take that step. It's just a matter of when. I'll wear you down Keegan. I'll have you panting and wet to the point you're beggin' me to take you."

Looking at Rage, I know he's dead serious. His plan is going to be to get me to the point that I go to him. He's not going to make the first move, other than his amazing kisses. If anything happens between us, I am going to have to make the first move. I know that he's leaving everything up to me in this area. He might be waiting a while, but then again, he might not.

We're sitting on the couch watching *Sweet Home Alabama*, one of my favorite movies. Rage is sitting with my head in his lap, an arm around me, and a blanket covering me. The only way I'll watch movies is covered up. Even if it's a hundred degrees out, I'll be covered up in a light blanket. This is something that I've done from the time I was a little girl. One of my nannies started it and I just continued doing it once she was fired for getting too close to me.

"You awake?" Rage asks, rubbing his hand up and down my arm.

"I am. I won't fall asleep during this movie."

Rage continues to rub up and down my arm, gently grazing the side of my breast. I know he can feel the trembling in my body and that he's having an affect on me. I always feel things I don't want to whenever he's near. He knows this, even when I don't want him to.

"What are you doing to me, Rage?" I ask him, turning my head up to face him.

"The same thing that you're doin' to me," he answers honestly.

I smile up at him and let him see that I don't mind the effect he has on me. I'm going to try to resist it as much as I can, but I don't hate it. If he has his way though, I'll be giving up and submitting to him very soon. It wouldn't necessarily be a bad thing, I just don't want them caught up in my drama. If Riley weren't in a location I'd already lived in, I'd be leaving to go see her very soon.

"I can see the thoughts whirlin' in your head babe," Rage says, tipping my head back further. "You're not leavin'. If you try, I'll find you and bring you back here quicker than you can blink."

Sitting up, I straddle his lap. I can feel how hard he is, and I honestly want nothing more than to release him and let him do what he wants to me. It would be the easiest thing in the world to do. And, it doesn't hurt that it's what we both want.

"If I want to leave, I'm going to leave. There's nothing anyone can do about it," I tell him, grinding down on him. "Rage, I want you more than I can tell you or show you. But, there's too much working against us right now."

"There's nothin' workin' against us. It's all in your head," Rage tells me. "And if you don't stop grindin' down on me like that, you'll be gettin' more than you bargained for. I can promise you that."

"And you think you can do better than what I've already had?" I ask, poking the bear.

"I know I can. You got one more chance baby. One more word like that and I'm goin' to show you exactly what I can do," Rage tells me, and I know he's serious. I just can't seem to help myself though.

"I think you're all talk big man," I tell him, wanting what he has and not being able to stop myself anymore.

"I warned you, now you're goin' to see," he tells me.

Before I can blink, Rage has me in his arms and is leading me to the bedroom I sleep in. I figured that we'd just do this on the couch, apparently, I was wrong. As soon as he slams the door shut with his foot, Rage has me on the bed and is on top of me. His hands are roaming my body and he's kissing me breathless once again.

"I can't wait to see all of you," he tells me.

No sooner are the words out of his mouth and Rage is stripping me out of my clothes. At the same time, I'm trying to maneuver to get his clothes off him. If he gets to see me naked, then I get to see him naked too. Finally, I have his shirt off and I stare down at his amazing body. My gaze travels from his chest down to his six pack. I can't help licking my lips, wanting to taste him.

I don't even realize that he's already got my shirt off until I feel his hand sneaking behind my back to unhook my bra. There's nothing I want to do more right now than to hide my body from his gaze. I don't have the scars that Whitney has told me she has, but I don't like the way I look. I know I need to put more weight on and I have bones sticking out where they shouldn't.

"You're not hidin' from me," he tells me, grabbing my hands in one of his and holding them above my head. "I want to see all that is you and look for as long as I want to. You're gonna let me Keegan."

"But, I know that I need to gain weight and I don't like it right now."

"You let me worry about that," he says, leaning down to kiss me again.

Rage starts to make his way down to my chest. He's nipping, kissing, and licking to where he wants to go. When he reaches my nipple, I arch up into him, letting him know what I want without using words. He doesn't need any words though. Rage knows exactly what I want and he's playing my body like a finely tuned instrument. He's not even letting me touch him. Every time I go to move my hands to put them on him, he gives me a look and I immediately still. There's no way I want him to stop doing anything he's doing right now.

Rage makes his way down my body, finishing removing my clothes as he goes. By the time he gets between my legs, where I want him the most, I'm squirming as much as I can on the bed. He is absolutely driving me insane. Instead of zeroing in where I want him the most, Rage takes his time getting to my pussy and I'm about to scream before he finally does. Usually, I don't like anyone going down on me, but Rage isn't going to give me a choice in the matter. And he knows what he's doing. In just a few minutes of him using his tongue and fingers on me, I'm finding my first release. He doesn't give me a chance to come down though.

While I'm still coming down from the best orgasm I've ever had, Rage slowly enters me. I don't get a chance to touch him, or even see how big he is. Instead, I'm going to have to feel how big he is. Not that I'm complaining. I can tell he's not all the way in and I already feel so full.

I'm getting tired of waiting for him as he takes his time. So, I surge up and make the rest of him go in. For a minute, neither one of us move. We just get used to one another. When I can't stand it anymore, I start to slowly move my hips to let him know I'm ready for him to continue.

Rage takes that as all the sign he needs to start pounding into me. There is no slow and gentle right now. He's giving me everything he has to give, and I want more. He isn't even on the bed with me, he's pulled me to the end of the bed while he stands.

I know that he doesn't want me to touch him, but there's no way I'm not going to touch myself. So, I run one of my hands down my body until I get to my clit. I'm so close to cumming again, I just need a little push over the edge. Since he doesn't say anything, I continue to roll and pinch my clit. Every now and then, I move my hand a little lower and wrap my fingers around him as he slides in and out. I can hear him growl when I do this and his hips jerk in response. Yeah, he's close and tryin to hold on to what control he has right now.

"Give it to me," he growls out.

I continue to play with myself and move my hips a little bit faster, adding a little twist to them. This only makes Rage lose a little bit more of his control and his moves become erratic. Now, I know that he's on the brink of finding his own release. He's just holding off until I find my second one, so I pinch my clit and feel my release run rampant through my body.

"Rage!" I yell out.

"Storm!" is the name that comes from his lips as he finds his release.

Instead of feeling euphoric from having another mind-blowing orgasm, I'm left feeling cold. I want nothing more than for him to get off me, but he has other ideas. Rage lands on me and rolls us to our side. He wants to hold me as we come down. I want to escape into my bathroom. Especially when I feel the first tear run down my cheek. I'm not going to cry in front of him. He won't see the pain and dread that is now filling my body.

As I go to move, I can feel his release sliding down my legs. I can't even say anything about it though. I'm too stunned and upset right now. The only thing I can think of is that I hope nothing results in this. I'm not on birth control and we obviously didn't use anything.

Rage couldn't understand why I didn't want him to hold me when we were done. I made up some excuse and escaped into the bathroom. As soon as the door was closed, I locked it, and made sure that he wouldn't be able to hear me crying. This meant that the music was blaring, and the shower was running. I just sat in the shower while listening to *The Best Of Me* by *Brantley Gilbert*.

I don't know who Storm is, but I'm not her. What the fuck? Apparently, this whole time, Rage has really wanted another woman. I'm not sure why she isn't with him or what's keeping them apart. All I know is that I'm not going to be a replacement for anyone. If Storm is who he wants, then Storm is who he can have. I guess my time here has come to an end. I'll miss my family, but I need to worry about me.

Chapter Two

Rage

I DON'T KNOW WHAT HAPPENED a month and a half ago to make Keegan leave. All I know is I got to spend one amazing night with her and then she disappeared as soon as I fell asleep. Ever since then, I've been searching all over for her.

"Rage, you still haven't found your girl?" Tank asks, coming up to sit with me.

"No. Why do you want to know?" I ask, snapping at him.

"I might have figured out what happened. I overheard some of the girls talkin'."

"What did they say? Do they know where she is?" I ask, perking up for the first time since she left.

"I don't know where she is, but I know why she left. Apparently, when you got off you screamed out Storm's name. Not hers," he tells me, letting me have a minute to absorb that information.

I sit there and think about that night. Keegan was as perfect as I knew she would be. There's times I like it a little rough and Keegan wanted me to give her what I had in me to give. She not only wanted it, but she pushed back just as hard. When I finally lost control, I remember calling out a name. I just don't remember... Fuck! I did call out Storm's name.

"I'm guessin' by the look on your face that you remember doin' it," Tank says, seeing what no one wants him to see

"I did call out her name. What the fuck am I supposed to do now? There's only four weeks to go until

Sam and her dad come lookin' for her. If they haven't already found her."

"I don't know what to tell you. The only one that is gonna know where she is will be Whitney or Sami. I'm not even sure she told them where she is."

"I need to find out," I say, getting up and starting for the door.

Whitney should be home, but they've been working on opening up the bakery and store. It's the afternoon, so I know she's not at the diner. Making my way over to her house, I hope she can give me good news. I need to know where Keegan is and explain who Storm is. I'm sure the girls have already told Whitney.

Knocking on the door, I can hear laughter and talking coming from the back of the house. So, I make my way out there to see if it's Whitney or Sami. Rounding the corner, I see Whitney and the rest of the old ladies. This is going to be an interesting conversation to have in front of everyone. But, if it means keeping Keegan safe and getting her back then I'll suck it up and do it.

"What do you want Rage?" Bailey asks me.

"I need to talk to Whitney," I respond.

"About what?" Whitney asks. "Keegan?"

"Yeah."

"And why would I talk to you about her after you chased her away? You made her leave and she's not coming back. Because you don't know who you want. She's not one to play games with."

"I'm not playin' games. Storm has been on my mind because of the way I feel about Keegan. If the girls have filled you in, then you know who Storm is. If not, then Storm is someone that used to be around the club.

She was killed and is no longer around. We were close, but we didn't make it past a friendship. So, Keegan is bringin' up things that I don't want to feel right now. Especially with the threat of her dad and Sam."

"They told me who Storm is. And, I've already tried to tell Keegan that. As far as she's concerned though, you still want Storm and are going to be chasing her until the day you die. She's always going to be the one you want."

"That's not true at all," I tell them. "Keegan is the one that I want. She's the one that's makin' me feel the way I do. Every day, when I'm not on club business, I'm starin' at the picture of the two of us that Kasey took. I see myself spendin' my life gettin' to know her. Whitney, if you know where she is, please tell me. I'm beggin' you," I tell her, not bothering to hide the fact that I'm pleading with her. Hell, I'll get down on my knees if I have to.

"All I'm gonna say is call Slim. And if you think about fucking her over, I'll beat the shit out of you. Well, I'll try to anyway," Whitney tells me. "I'm serious when I say don't fuck with her. Rage, I want her here with us. She needs to be around her family."

"I give you my word. Thank you, Whitney."

I make my way back to the clubhouse so that I can call Slim. If he knows where she is then that means she's in Benton Falls. There's only one reason she would know about them and that's because the girls knew she was leaving. It kind of pisses me off that no one said anything to me. Especially when they knew how hard I was searching for her.

I've talked to Slim and Grim. I'm now packing Kasey and I up to head to Benton Falls for a few days. We're going to surprise Keegan and make sure that she comes home with us. She needs to hear a few things regarding Storm. Am I playing dirty by taking Kasey with me? Absolutely! Do I care at this point? Nope. I want to get Keegan back to the house and get back on track with where we were heading. If I have to grovel and beg her for forgiveness, then that's what I'll do. There's not much I won't do to make sure my girl comes home where she belongs.

"Daddy, are we bringing Keegan home?" Kasey asks me, pulling her bag behind her.

"Yeah sweet pea, we are," I tell her.

"Good. I miss her. She's fun daddy."

"I miss her too," I tell my daughter honestly. "Now, we're gonna have a long drive, so do you want books or anythin'?"

"I got them daddy. I'm ready to go."

Kasey and I make our way out to the truck. I fasten her in and see Grim and Bailey making their way towards us. I really don't want to talk to anyone right now, but he is my President, so I need to hear what he has to say.

"If you see anythin', you let Slim know and then call me. Is that understood?" he asks me.

"I will. My main priority is to protect these two with everythin' I am."

"Are you sure about this, Rage?" Bailey asks me.

"I am. I know it hasn't been a long time, but I know it in my heart that Keegan is the one for me. The way that Irish feels about Whitney is the same way I feel about Keegan."

"And what about Keegan. Does she feel the same?" she asks.

"I think she does. We're about to find out, aren't we?"

"Let us know when you get there, Rage," Grim tells me.

I nod in acknowledgment and get in the truck. Bailey kisses and hugs Kasey goodbye before we can finally be on our way to our future. There's no way that I'll accept anything less than Keegan coming back with us. This is where she belongs and it's up to me to bring her back.

Keegan

The night I spent with Rage was one of the best I've ever had. Well, up until he called out another woman's name. Whitney and the rest of the girls have tried to explain to me who Storm was, but I'm not hearing it. There's no way I can compete with a ghost. I won't be anyone's second choice. I've spent too many years running and hiding to be made to feel less than what I am. I know what I'm worth and one day someone will see that.

Slim and his club have been amazing. Bailey and Whitney were the first two to know that I was leaving. Bailey made the arrangements for me to come and stay with the Phantom Bastards. It's been a blast. Wood and Boy Scout have been by my side since I got here.

At first, I thought something was off with them. We went out a few times and I saw them checking out the girls. That's not the strange part. The part that confused me in the beginning was overhearing them talking about sharing women. I thought they had some bisexual relationship going on. Which I don't have a problem with at all. They explained to me that they share women and not one another. It's never been physical between them. It's just them sharing one woman. Trust me, I'm very interested in finding out what that's all about. Too bad Rage won't leave my mind.

"So, are we gonna play cards or what Keegan?" Boy Scout asks me.

"Yeah. Let me just get the cookies from the oven and I'll be right in."

A few nights a week, the guys and I play cards, watch movies, or just hang out talking. That's after they've spent all day standing guard. On these nights, I either cook for them or we order takeout. It's a blast and I usually end up in fits of laughter. Especially the night they tried to talk me into going to a club with them. They wanted to go find a piece of ass and decided that I'd make the perfect wingman. I'm not sure why, but they were hilarious in their attempts. It also didn't hurt that Slim vetoed the idea when he said that I shouldn't be exposed when we didn't know where my dad and Sam were hiding.

"What kind of cookies firefly?" Wood asks, bringing in beer for them and soda for me.

"Chocolate chip. Well, they're not really cookies. So, you can't touch the pan until I'm completely done with it. It's gotta cool and then I add stuff to them."

"You're really gonna make us wait?" Boy Scout pouts.

"I know you're pouting in there, Boy Scout. If you keep it up, you won't get anything at all. Pull up your big boy pants and deal with it," I tell him, letting the smile spread across my face.

I can hear Wood's laughter and I know that Boy Scout is turning red. Yeah, he may be a badass biker, but he still blushes every now and then. It's cute and endearing. Now I know that when I get in there, he's going to do something to get pay back. These two are like brothers I never had and didn't necessarily want.

Walking in to the living room, I see they've already set the table up and Wood is dealing the cards out. I'm guessing that we're going to be playing our standard game of poker. Too bad I don't know how to play. If we played strip poker, I'd be naked in a matter of seconds. Wood suggested that one night and I thought Boy Scout was going to choke on his beer. He was trying so hard not to laugh, but it didn't necessarily work. Wood may have ended up covered in beer before too long.

"Poker again guys?" I ask.

"You know it," Wood tells me, smiling his wolfish smile.

I sit down so we can play, and the guys take my mind off anything that may be on it. We play for an hour and a half and I finally decide to put Boy Scout out of his misery. Walking into the kitchen, I pull out the peanut butter and chocolate frosting. I made chocolate chip cookies into brownies. Now, I'm going to put a layer of peanut butter on them and then finish it off with chocolate frosting. Riley used to love these things. Kasey loves them too.

Boy Scout isn't far behind me. He always keeps me company in the kitchen. Mainly because he wants to be the first one to get whatever I'm making. It doesn't matter if I'm baking or cooking. If I'm honest, I think that if he had the choice, Wood wouldn't get anything to eat while they're here.

"Are they done yet?" Boy Scout asks, reminding me of an over-eager little boy waiting for a surprise.

"Almost. If you don't calm down, I'm going to give the first piece to Wood and not you."

"That's not fair firefly," he tells me, sitting down in the chair at the table. Wood isn't far behind him.

Finally done, I cut them each a piece of the brownies. They gobble them down without taking a breath. I can't help but double over in laughter at watching them eat. It's like they haven't eaten in days. Maybe months. I know for a fact that they had dinner because I had beef stew cooking in the crockpot all day. Then I made crescent rolls to go with it.

This is how my days now go. I almost wouldn't change anything about it. But, Rage and Kasey aren't here. They are the ones that I want to be spending my time with. I'm just not going to be some sort of replacement for him. He's going to have to decide what he truly wants, then he can make a play for me. If that's what he chooses.

Today, they're taking me to the doctor. I haven't been feeling very good and they want to make sure that no one's tampered with anything I've come into contact with. Not only did I explain the situation, but Grim also called and talked to them. Thankfully, my dad hasn't found me yet because I haven't received any letters or flowers since I left Clifton Falls. I'm not sure if they're still going there or not. Whitney hasn't mentioned it and I haven't asked.

"Firefly, are you ready to go?" Wood asks, coming in my room.

"Yeah. As ready as I'll ever be I guess."

"Boy Scout is waiting to lock up and arm the alarm system."

We make our way outside and I get in the car I just bought. I've been working at the local restaurant and my tips and paychecks allowed me to buy a car. Especially when Slim won't let me pay rent or anything else. We've had many arguments about it and I've lost every single time. I thought Rage was bossy, but he's got nothing on Slim when he doesn't want to budge on something. He takes bossy to whole new level. Shy is the only one I see that gives it right back to him. Those two are so funny to watch when they get going.

Wood has been driving my car while Boy Scout follows behind us. It gives me a peace of mind to know that I'm still being protected, but I can't wait for the day that I can go out on my own without having to worry. When this is all done, I'll be able to go out without having to look over my shoulder all the time. I won't have to worry about those that I love and care about getting hurt just to get to me. Hopefully I get to see the day that it gets taken care of.

"Let me know if I have to pull over firefly," Wood tells me.

There may have been an instance that I threw up in his truck. We were heading back from the clubhouse and I couldn't wait. I had no time to tell him to pull over or to roll the window down. When he told me not to worry about cleaning his truck, I knew I couldn't do that. So, the next day, I spent the entire day cleaning his truck out. He managed to get most of it done after making sure I got in bed. I just made sure to finish it and detail the rest of the truck while I was at it.

It doesn't take that long to get to the doctor's office. Thankfully. Wood follows me in while Boy Scout wait's outside with the car. I go to the window and give them my name. The receptionist hands me a bunch of papers to fill out before giving her attention to the person behind me.

Walking over to Wood, I sit down to fill out the papers I've done dozens of times before. This is what I hate because I have to give my name and I don't want to do anything that would cause my dad or Sam to find me. This time I'll just have to suck it up and take my chances though. Two weeks of being sick is too long not to get checked out. At first, I thought I had caught the flu since it's getting cold outside. Then I thought it could be from all the stress of not knowing when my dad and Sam will strike. Now, I don't think it's either of those things.

Before I'm done filling out all of the papers, which are repetitive I might add, a nurse calls me back. Wood stands up to follow me back and I go to stop him. Instead of sitting back down and waiting for me, he cocks an eyebrow and doesn't say a word. I guess this is his way of letting me know that I'm not leaving his sight.

After doing everything the nurse asks me to do, I finally make it in to a room and sit on the table while Wood sit's in the only chair in the room. She takes my vitals and then tells me to wait on the doctor. Before she makes it out of the room, I'm lunging for the garbage can. This is bullshit and I'm so tired from getting sick all the time. Hopefully today they can figure out what's wrong and give me what I need to make this stop.

Wood holds my hair back and then helps me back on the exam table when I'm done getting sick. It always drains me, and I just want to take a nap. I'll have to wait until I can get back to the house. As I lay back on the table, Wood finds paper towels that he wets down and puts on my forehead. This is the same stuff he does whenever he catches me getting sick. He's such a sweetheart and I can't wait until Boy Scout and him can find their own woman.

"Good morning Keegan," the doctor says walking through the door. "I'm Doctor Sanchez."

"Morning," I mutter in reply.

"It says here that you haven't been feeling very good for a few weeks. Let's see what your chart says. Well, it looks like you don't have the flu or anything. It looks like you're pregnant," she says, setting the chart down.

"What did you just say?" I ask, astonished beyond belief right now. "You must have someone else's chart in your hand."

"I'm sorry Keegan, this is definitely your chart. I take it this wasn't expected," she says, the sympathy pouring out of her.

"No, it wasn't expected," I tell her, looking over to Wood. "You can't tell anyone. Promise me, Wood."

"I can't promise anythin' firefly."

"Why do you call me firefly?" I ask, even though this really isn't the time to be talking about this.

"From the night you sat outside catchin' fireflies when you first got here. I've never seen anyone sit there for hours tryin' to catch them."

"Well, it was more about thinking and trying to figure things out. Not necessarily about catching fireflies."

Wood shrugs his shoulders and I know that I have a nickname from him and Boy Scout. I'm not sure if it's going to catch on with anyone else for the club, but I'll go with whatever right now. Doctor Sanchez explains what I'll have to do during the rest of the pregnancy, gives me some pamphlets and scripts for vitamins and anti-nausea medicine, and then tells me she'll see me in a month.

We walk back to the car and I can't believe what I just found out. The one-time Rage and I are together, and I get pregnant. How the fuck does that happen to me? It must be something telling me to go back to Clifton Falls. There's no way that I'm going to keep Rage's baby from him. I guess we're all getting what we want. Even if I'm scared shitless for multiple reasons.

No matter how much I fought against being with Rage, I've always wanted him. For once in my life I could see myself settling down and being with someone. Rage is the only one that brought that out in me. The only reason I left is because of him calling out Storm's name. To me, it meant that he wanted someone else and I was just filling his time until she became his.

"You good firefly?" Wood asks as he helps me in my car.

"Um, I don't honestly know. I think I just want to go to the house and take a nap. You guys can go do whatever it is you need to do."

"No can do. We'll be right by your side until you know what you wanna do," he tells me, closing me in the car and heading to the driver's side.

I'm still trying to wrap my head around the fact that I'm about to have a baby in a few months. Yeah, I'm probably only a month and a half pregnant, but I bet the next seven and a half months are going to fly by. Or, they'll drag by because Rage is going to be a caveman and try to make me do what he wants me to do. I can see him trying to make me rest and do as little as possible for most of this pregnancy. Ha! That's not going to happen.

When I laid down, I only wanted to sleep for a little bit. Waking up, I realize that I've slept for about four hours. Damn! Now, the day is gone and everything I wanted to do is going to have to be pushed to tomorrow. I guess tomorrow is going to be a busy as hell day.

Before I can register anything else, I have to run to the bathroom. Usually Wood comes rushing in when he can hear me getting sick. Today, the last person I ever thought would be here is by my side. Rage is holding my hair, rubbing my back, and letting the water run so he can give me a cool cloth. I can't even question why he's here right now.

Finally, I'm done, and Rage leads me back into the bedroom. I sit on the edge of the bed and look up at Rage. Damn, the man is even sexier than I remember. He's looking down at me, concern written all over his face. Now, I know that I'm going to have to explain what's going on. Fuck! Why can't this day be over already? I don't want to have to deal with this right now.

"Are you okay?" he asks me.

"Yeah. Nothing I haven't been dealing with for a little bit now," I tell him, trying to purposely be vague.

"What's goin' on Keegan? You used to tell me things."

"I don't want to tell you right now. I've barely wrapped my head around it and now you're going to know. But, I can't hide it from you either."

Rage sits down next to me and waits for me to open up to him. This is hard. Especially when I don't know how he's going to react about having a baby. We've never talked about it and we never really talked about what was going to happen between us. Sure, he's said that I was going to be in his life forever, or however he said it, but we never talked about what that meant. I guess that's about to be discussed now too.

"So, I'm guessing that Wood told you I've been sick?" I ask him, not knowing how to start this conversation.

"He did. But, what I want to know is why you ran away? Especially without comin' to me first."

"You called out another woman's name the one and only time we were together Rage. I don't know hardly anything about you, yet you continue to tell me we're going to be around one another for a long time. I don't even know what that means. There's too many what-ifs and I'm not going to be anyone's second choice," I tell him, feeling the tears building already.

"I know baby, and I'm sorry as fuck about it. Storm was a girl that was in the club as a club girl. Summer and her have helped the old ladies more than anyone else and we became close. When I brought Kasey home, she was one of the main ones that helped me out with her. I thought we were headin' to somethin' more than friends until she was killed. I went off the rails when she died and disappeared for a little while. Part of that was tryin' to take out the people that took her out. The other part of that was losin' control. I started drinkin' and other shit just to numb myself from the pain. Kasey is the one that suffered," he tells me. "The more time I spend with you, the more I realized that what I felt for Storm was nothin'. She had been on my mind a lot and that's why I called out her name. It wasn't because I want her still. I'm not chasin' some ghost. I want you, and only you."

I take in what he's just told me, and I know that he's not lying. It doesn't mean that it doesn't hurt any less, I just know that he's confused. On one hand, he still wants to know what would've happened with Storm. On the other hand, he's happy that she's not here so he can explore whatever this is that we have. I would be confused as hell too. Especially if they were as close as what everyone is saying.

"Rage, I understand where you're coming from. It's just going to take some time for me to wrap my head around it. Can you understand that?" I ask.

"I get it baby. Now, why did Wood take you to the doctor? What's goin' on with you?" he asks. "I'm assumin' it has somethin' to do with you bein' sick a little while ago."

"It does. I haven't been feeling too good lately and decided that I needed to get checked out. Well, it turns out that I'm going to be feeling like this for a little while."

"What do you have baby?"

"I'm pregnant Rage. The one and only time we were together got me pregnant," I tell him, waiting to hear what he's going to say.

For a few minutes, he says absolutely nothing. Now, my mind is racing with all the possible thoughts going through his head. He probably thinks that I'm trying to trap him with a baby or something. That's so far from the truth though. We were both there and I had as much responsibility for not using protection as he did. It never even crossed my mind honestly because I wanted him so bad in that moment.

"Okay. Well, I guess that certainly changes things a bit then," he murmurs. "What are you goin' to do?"

"I'm keeping the baby. You don't have to be a part of its life. We don't need to be together or anything. You know that I'm pregnant and we can figure out where to go from here. I'm perfectly capable of raising the baby on my own and you can visit him or her as much as you want to. I don't want anything from you Rage," I tell him, trying to sound as confident as I can.

"Yeah, I'm goin' to be a part of the baby's life alright. On an everyday basis Keegan. We're goin' to do this and be together. You're comin' home, do what you gotta do to wrap your head around that baby."

I sit in stunned silence. In all honesty, I didn't think that Rage was going to be all gun ho about us being together. And, I'm sure as hell not going to be with him because of the baby. No matter how hot the sex might get. We're going to have to take some time and figure out if this is what we truly want. Just as I go to tell him my feelings on the matter, I hear footsteps running down the hall towards us.

"Kasey, why don't you let your dad and firefly talk for a little bit. Then they'll come out and play with you," I hear Wood say.

"Who is firefly?" Rage and Kasey ask at the same time.

"Keegan's nickname from me is firefly," he says, entering the doorway.

"And why the fuck are you givin' my girl a nickname?" Rage asks, letting the anger show.

"Um…Well, you weren't here, and she sat outside collectin' fireflies in a jar for hours," he answers like it's no big deal.

"If anyone is givin' her a name, it's gonna be me," Rage says, getting off the bed and heading towards Wood. "Kasey, why don't you go see Boy Scout for a few minutes sweet pea?"

"Is Wood in trouble daddy? You have your mean face on."

"We're just gonna have a chat," Rage tells his sweet little girl.

"Okay. I'm gonna have Boy Scout push me on the swing out back."

With that, Kasey goes running off to find Boy Scout. I stay rooted to the bed and wait to see what's going to happen between Wood and Rage. This isn't going to end well for him if Rage is anything like Crash and Trojan. But, I'm going to let them settle it between themselves. If I've learned anything, it's to let the men do what they do and then sort it all out after the fact. This situation is no different.

"Now, even if I weren't around, what makes you think you can give her a nickname? You better make it good Wood," Rage says, taking the last few steps towards him.

"Listen, no disrespect meant Rage. She ended up sittin' out there for hours thinkin' of nothin' but you and how much she was missin' you. Yes, Keegan, I know that's exactly what you were doin'. I don't know why I started callin' her firefly, I just did and now I barely call her Keegan. I'm sorry Rage."

"You're lucky that I like you and I think you receive enough abuse from Crash and Trojan. Otherwise, I'd be beatin' the livin' fuck out of you right now. I might even start callin' her that myself. I kind of like that name for her."

Rage actually shocks the shit out of me. I figured he was going to beat the shit out of Wood and now he's going to start calling me firefly too. Who would've thought that someone else giving me a nickname would stick with so many people? I certainly didn't. Just like I have no clue how Wood knew I was sitting there pining away for Rage when I never opened my mouth about him to anyone here. Word must travel fast through these clubs.

"Now that we have the pissing match out of the way. There's a little girl that wants some attention. And please, I want to keep this between the three of us for right now. After what I told you happened before Rage, I don't want to jinx anything."

"Whatever you want firefly," Rage answers. Oh boy!

"I won't say a word to anyone. I don't need Rage beatin' the shit out of me."

The three of us make our way out to the back of the house where Boy Scout and Kasey are. She's swinging and giggling without a care in the world. Boy Scout is laughing with her and it's like he hasn't laughed in years. I've never seen him so relaxed and at peace. Six weeks is a long time to go without seeing him like that. But, he's been on guard duty and has taken that seriously. Almost as bad as Rage has been with me.

"Keegannnnnn!" Kasey hollers. "Come play with me. I've missed you so much!"

"I've missed you too sweetheart," I tell her making my way to the swings.

Rage follows me over and I know that he's going to be the one to push me on the swing. He's not going to let anyone else get close to me now that he's here. This should be interesting. Wood just hangs back and pulls up a chair, so he can keep an eye on things while we're having fun.

"Daddy, can you get Keegan higher than me?" Kasey asks. "I bet you can't!"

"Is that a challenge sweet pea?"

"Yep."

I don't know if my stomach will let me go as high as Rage is going to push me, but we'll find out. Hopefully, if I have to get sick, I can at least make it to the bathroom so Kasey doesn't have to see it. I don't need her getting upset or worried because she thinks I'm sick.

And, I'm going to follow Rage's lead as far as when she gets told we're having a baby. She's his daughter and he needs to make that decision.

"You ready for this firefly?" he asks, pulling the swing back.

"I don't know how high I can go Rage. Just take that into consideration. I don't want to get sick in front of her," I let him know quietly.

"I know baby. I got you."

Rage acts like he's going to give me one hell of a push. Instead he just lets me go and I start swinging at the same pace as Kasey. She's laughing so hard that Rage isn't making me go higher than her and I can't help but join in the laughter. Unfortunately, my stomach chooses this moment to have other ideas about what I need to be doing. So, I quickly stop the swing and make a beeline for the house. I can hear Kasey asking what's wrong and Rage making up a story.

Thankfully, I make it to the bathroom in time and it's not long before Rage makes his way in to me. Just like before, he takes care of me. It's the little things he does that make him so special. And I know that he's not like this with everyone. Sure, there's loyalty and respect with his brothers and their old ladies. But, the sweet soft side is reserved for Kasey and me. It's just taken me a little bit to see that.

"I think I'm good now," I tell him, hauling myself up off the floor.

After brushing my teeth, we make our way back outside and I sit in the seat that Wood vacated at some point. Kasey is still swinging, and Boy Scout is still pushing her. Rage takes a seat next to me and I know that he's worried already about me being sick. There's nothing I can do about it though. Not until I go back to the doctor in a month. I'll just take the pills she gave me and hope they help control the nausea a little bit. Anything at this point would be better than feeling the way I do.

"You good firefly?" Rage asks me.

"Yeah. I'm just really tired again. It takes a lot out of me and I just want to take a nap."

"So, go take one. Kasey has her stuff in one of the spare bedrooms already. I'm sleepin' in your room. We're fine to hang out while you get some sleep," he tells me, kissing the back of my hand.

"Are you sure? I should be fine in a little bit."

"Go. We'll order somethin' for dinner and make sure to save you some. I know how these two can eat."

After giving him a kiss and telling Kasey that I'll see her in a little bit, I head inside. Wood is standing in the kitchen, holding a glass of water for me. He's so used to taking care of me after a month and a half that it's just second nature to him. Plus, I think he wants to make sure that Rage knows I have options out there. And if he doesn't watch his step, there will be someone that wants to take his place. Not that I'd let that happen, but it's nice to know that Wood cares.

Once again, I've slept for longer than I wanted to. I can hear everyone in the living room talking and laughing. It sounds like there's more than just the four that were here when I came in for a nap. Not that I want to hang out with a lot of people right now. I guess it is what it is, and I don't have much of a choice. So, I make myself look presentable and head out there.

"There's sleepin' beauty," Boy Scout says.

I give everyone a slight smile and head into the kitchen. There's pizza, wings, and cheesy garlic bread on the counter and I help myself to some of it. Slim, Playboy, and Killer are here, and I wonder what's going on. Other than a check-in every now and then, I haven't seen Slim or anyone else from the club. Hell, I won't even go to the clubhouse. I've been there two times in the month and a half I've been here. The first time was when I arrived in Benton Falls, and the other one was when Wood had to run there really quick.

"So, what did I miss?" I ask, leaning against Rage and taking my first bite of pizza.

"Nothin' much firefly," Slim says.

He starts laughing when I about choke on my food and my eyes bug out at his use of my nickname. Rage is frantically pounding on my back to make sure that I don't choke, and the rest of the men are standing around looking at the crazy chick. Who knew the President of an MC would be calling me a name Wood started. Yep, it's definitely going to be sticking for sure now.

"You good baby?" Rage asks finally.

"Yeah. Just a shock is all."

"So, we were just talkin' and tryin' to figure out what your plans are," Slim tells me.

Fuck! I haven't had a chance to really decide what I wanted to do yet. Rage obviously is going to have to go back home but I don't know what I want. Honestly, my entire family is back in Clifton Falls. Whitney, Irish, and their kids are the only people I consider to be my family. The girls are back there. Here, there's not really any old ladies for me to talk to or get to know. So, I've been sticking to myself.

"Um…Do I have to decide right this second?" I ask after swallowing the mouthful of food.

"No. But, I'm goin' to let you know that the flowers are comin' here now too. Not sure how they found you, but they did. Boy Scout intercepted the delivery this mornin'."

"What's the card say?" I ask, the color draining from my body and the food I was eating threatening to come back up. "I need to know."

"Just tell her Slim. It's somethin' she feels she needs to know. So, I don't put up too much fight about it."

Slim reaches in his pocket and pulls the envelope out. With shaking hands, I take the card and just hold it for a minute. Even though I need to know what my father is saying, I don't want to know. It's been six weeks and I can just imagine what he's saying on this one. Finally, I decide that I can't put it off any longer and pull the card out. Before I open it up, I look around at the men in the room and gather strength from them.

Keegan,

You have wasted half of the time Sam gave you to come to him on your own. Instead, you up and disappear again. You're making us waste valuable resources to continually track you down, and Sam is done playing games. He's ready to cut your time down and make you come to him now. I'm going to say you have about a week left before we get you. This could've been so much easier for everyone if you just did what you were told to do.

Sincerely,

Your Loving Father

If he thinks that I'm letting them come take me away, they've got another thing coming. I'll run again and hide before I let that happen. These guys have no clue who they're dealing with. Carl and my uncle were pussies compared to Sam. Who do they think started this whole selling young girls to settle debts? It wasn't Carl or anyone else. Sam has been through about ten girls so far. And that was the last number I heard years ago.

"What's goin' through your head firefly?" Rage asks, wrapping his arms tight around me.

"Needing to run is at the top of the list. But, I'm not going to. I'm going to trust in you and the club to protect me."

"Good girl," Rage says.

"So, where are you gonna be livin'? I only ask because either we're goin' back with you, or they're comin' here," Slim says.

"What do you mean?" Rage asks.

"I mean, we don't know exactly what we're dealing with. From the intel we got, he's worse than we first thought. So, I talked to Grim and we decided that at least two clubs need to be present. Gage's club is busy dealin' with whatever Darcy has goin' on right now."

"What's going on with her?" I ask. I've only met her once or twice, but she's a sweet girl.

"No one knows for sure. She's bein' tight-lipped about it," Slim answers. "All we know is somethin' ain't right and they might need backup but we're more worried about you right this second."

"It's up to firefly," Rage tells me. "I'm gonna need to go back soon, and I really don't want to leave you. But, if the club comes here I won't have to leave. So, it's your call."

Way to leave this shit up to me! I have no clue what to do now. I mean, in Clifton Falls most of the families live behind the fence. Here, they don't have that. So, maybe it would be safer for us to go back there. Or maybe they have more gun power or something here. Fuck!

"Well, all I can say is that I think it should be up to you guys. You know who's better equipped. So, I'll go where you think the better place is."

"Then we'll head out in two hours back to Clifton Falls," Slim says. "That give you enough time to pack your stuff firefly?"

"Yeah. It's mainly clothes because I don't have anything else. I always had to travel light."

Everyone heads out except for Boy Scout. They wanted to leave more, but they all need to get ready to head out. Boy Scout said that Wood can take care of his stuff for him and he'll stand outside and make sure no one tries anything. Rage is in my room with me while Kasey makes sure all of her stuff is packed back up. Not that she had a lot of time to get anything out.

"You okay baby?" Rage asks, helping me pack my meager belongings up.

"Yeah. I mean as good as I can be with everything going on right now. I'm sorry this is coming to you guys. I should've made you let me go as soon as my uncle left."

"Wouldn't have happened. You should know that by now."

"I do know that. I'm just saying that me being around you all is bringing a ton of danger to you. It's not fair to everyone."

Rage holds me close for a few minutes. We don't talk or anything. I just listen to the beating of his heart and let it calm me down. He's the only one that can calm me when I feel like my world is crashing down around me. I'm not sure if it's because he got me out of the back of that car, or if it's because of whatever connection we have. All I know is that when he's holding me, all is right with the world.

"Let's get finished so we can head out. I want you back at the clubhouse before it gets too late. And you know you're goin' to have to answer questions about why you're sick, right?"

"I know. I'll just avoid them if I can. Say I ate something bad?"

"Don't think that will work when you barely eat. I noticed you only had a few bites and then quit eatin'. That's not gonna fly with me firefly. Especially with you carryin' our baby," Rage says.

Before we know it, there's a gasp coming from the door. We both whip our heads around and see Kasey standing there. She's heard that I'm having a baby and has a huge smile across her face. There's a twinkle in her eyes and I know she's excited.

"I'm gonna be a big sister?" she asks, coming in the room farther.

"You are," Rage answers. "But, you can't tell anyone. Can you help us keep this secret?"

"Yeah daddy. But why can't we tell?"

"Well, we just found out and we want to keep it to ourselves for a little bit. I promise when we want everyone to know, you can tell them," I tell Kasey.

She runs in and wraps her arms around our legs. This right here is what I've always longed for. I knew it would never happen if I was with Sam. Hopefully it doesn't get ripped away from me now that I've finally found Rage and Kasey.

Chapter Three

Rage

WE'VE BEEN BACK IN CLIFTON Falls for a few days. So far Kasey has kept our secret. It's getting hard to hide Keegan getting so sick on a regular basis. People are starting to notice. Well, the girls are starting to notice that she runs off on a regular basis. I think we need to have a talk and start letting people know what's going on.

"Rage, we need to talk," Whitney says, storming up to me.

"Okay. What's up?"

"I want to know what's going on with my cousin, and I want to know right fucking now!"

"What are you talkin' about?" I ask, deciding to play dumb.

"She's always running off to the bathroom. Then she's taking naps after the fact. If I didn't know any better, I would say she's pregnant," Whitney tells me, concern lacing her voice.

"Well, Whitney," Keegan says coming up behind her. "I am pregnant. We didn't want anyone to know just yet, so that's why we didn't tell you."

"Oh my! Are you serious?"

"I am. I just found out. Now, are you gonna keep this to yourself or am I gonna beat your ass?" my girl asks.

"I'll keep my mouth shut. I swear Keegan. Now, why is everyone calling you firefly?"

"Ask Wood," I growl out, still not liking the fact that Wood gave my girl a nickname.

Whitney looks between Keegan and me for a few minutes. Then, she shrugs her shoulders and starts to go in search of Irish. I take my girl by the hand and lead her to my room. I can tell from the look on her face that she thinks we're going to be talking. That's not what's going to go down right now. And she sees my intent as soon as I kick the door shut and throw the lock.

"Need you now," I tell her, leading her into the bathroom and turning on the shower.

"I'm here when you need me Rage," she answers.

"I want to hear my name come off your lips," I tell her, needing to hear my real name in her melodic voice. "It's Aiden."

"Aiden," she says shyly.

I groan in approval. My name has never sounded as sweet as it does coming from Keegan's mouth. My mother is the only other one to call me that and I want to hear it from Keegan when we're together. I have this need to hear it coming from her now. Keegan smiles up at me after groaning and starts removing her clothes. So, I check the temperature of the water before I undress.

"Aiden, I'm getting in now. You can join me when you get out of your head," she tells me, bringing me back to the present.

I hurry up removing the rest of my clothes and about bash my head on the sink. So, I take a minute to take in all that is Keegan standing under the water. Her long chestnut hair is plastered to her back as she smooths it away from her face. The water is cascading down her body and I want to lick and catch every drop. Finally, I can't stand it anymore, so I hop in the shower behind her and wrap my arms around her, pulling her body up against mine.

"Keegan, I need you to bend over and grab your ankles," I tell her, running my hands up and down her body.

There's no hesitation on her part. My girl bends over and grabs her ankles. I take her hair in my hand and move it off to the side so it's not falling in her face. Then, I run my fingers through her folds to see if she's wet enough for me to enter her. I can't wait to get inside her, and thankfully she's wet enough.

Sliding into her, I grab onto her hips so that she doesn't feel like she's going to fall forward. I never want her to feel anything but safe with me. Even when I'm pushing her limit's, I want her to know I'll never hurt her intentionally.

"Harder, Aiden," she moans out.

Not wanting to disappoint my girl, I give it to her harder. Keegan is always going to push me to my limit's, and I'm going to do the same to her. My grip on her hips gets tighter, and I push in and out faster and harder. Her moans get louder, and I don't care if anyone else hears her. I'm the only one that gets to see her, that gets to know what she likes and doesn't like. Things I'm still enjoying figuring out.

"Aiden, please, I need to cum," she moans out.

"Get it firefly," I tell her.

Keegan releases one of her ankles and moves her hand up to her clit. She plays with herself and pushes back against me even harder. I wish I could see what she's doing right now, see the look on her face. But, I don't want to change positions and make her lose being so close to her release. Hell, I'm close to finding my own.

Before I can manage more than a few more thrusts in and out, I feel Keegan's muscles clench around me. It feels better and better. Now, I know that I'm not going to last much longer. So, I take her hand away from her clit and move it back down towards her ankle to hang on. As soon as I know that she's back to holding on, I pound into her harder and faster than ever before. Honestly, I'm worried that I'm hurting her, but if the moans and gasps coming from her are anything to go by, I'd say my girl is enjoying it.

"Keegan!" I yell out as my release crashes through me.

After a few more gentle thrusts, I slump over her. I want nothing more than to hold her in my arms. But, we're in the shower and I know we need to clean up before heading to bed. It might not be bedtime just yet, but Keegan has been going to bed a little bit earlier than normal. She gets really tired most days and I'm more than happy to lay with her until she falls asleep. Especially knowing that she has a hard time falling asleep if I'm not in bed next to her. Then I'll get up and spend some time with Kasey before putting her back to bed. Our days are settling into a nice routine and I wouldn't change it for the world. Well, there's one thing I'd change. Us living in a house and not in my rooms at the clubhouse for the most part.

Keegan refuses to stay at Skylar's with us. She thinks that by doing that, we'll be bringing her dad and that asshat to their front door. Her main concern is the kids, but in reality, it's all of them. So, we stay at the clubhouse for now. I've already started making plans for our own home. It will be built close to Whitney's so that she's always near her cousin.

"Alright firefly, you get in bed and I'll be right there," I tell her after I dry her off.

I don't know if it's normal for her to be so tired all the time. I've seen the women go through their pregnancies and the only ones I saw that tired were Skylar and Maddie. The others were tired, but not like my girl. It's to the point that I'm getting really concerned and I'm going to have to call Doctor Sanchez to find out.

"Okay. You know, you don't have to get in bed with me," she tells me, already heading for the bed.

"Yeah, I do. I know you don't sleep good if I'm not in bed with you. Kasey knows what's goin' on and she likes that I make sure you're asleep before I go to her. The only thing she said that would make it better were if we were to tuck her into bed together."

"Well, then I'll stay up so we can do that," she says, going over to get dressed.

"No. Get in bed and I'll be right there. You'll get there, baby."

Keegan finally gets in bed and I'm thankful to see her almost asleep as soon as her head hit's the pillow. Before I call the doctor, I think I'll talk to Skylar and Maddie. Kasey is with them right now. Then, I'll take care of Kasey and play with her before finding something for Keegan to eat when she wakes up. Whitney told me to get her crackers and to try dry toast. She said it helped her so it's worth a shot for my girl.

"Daddy! Daddy!" Kasey calls out, rounding the corner from the main room. "You gotta come with me."

Kasey is so excited about something and I can't help but wonder what it is. It's been a long time since I've seen her this worked up over anything. So, I'm practically jogging as I follow my daughter to the main room. Once we get there, I see everyone moving around in quick order.

"Come on daddy! You're too slow!" Kasey calls out again.

She leads me to the door and what I see steals my breath away. I knew it was getting cold outside, but it's now snowing. I'm not talking about a few flurries floating down, it's almost a whiteout right now. So, I run out to help put the bikes in the garage. We added on to it so that we could store our bikes in the cold weather.

"It's been so long since it's snowed here," Skylar says, walking outside. "We typically get some but not this early."

"Are they sayin' anythin' on the news or radio?" Grim asks no one in particular.

"Not much. I guess it's a surprise for everyone," Glock answers. "I'll keep it on so we know what we're in for."

"Guess it's a good thing we just went shopping," Bailey says, joining us outside.

As soon as the bikes are all put up, we head back in to see everyone watching the snow fall. I have to admit that it's amazing to watch it cover everything in a blanket of pure white. It's almost as if it's cleansing everything so that we can all start over. Especially when the ground is already covered and it's sticking to everything else. We might have to go out tomorrow to get whatever we need to clear it out of the parking lot and make sure everyone can get to their houses.

"Tomorrow, Rage, Tank, and Joker I want you to go out and buy every shovel you can find. We're gonna need all hands-on deck to get this cleaned up. Glock, I want you to price some four wheelers or something like that so we can be better prepared next time this happens. We're gonna need to make sure there's enough winter wear for everyone here. Including the Phantom

Bastards," Grim tells everyone. "You got anythin' else Slim?"

"Nope. I think if people are leaving the clubhouse then we need to make sure that they watch everythin' surroundin' them. We don't know when this asshole is goin' to make a move, and he might choose now to do so. He'll think we're panicked and try somethin'."

"Good point. Firefly is to stay in someone's eye sight at all times," Grim says, looking directly at me.

"Um," Keegan says, coming out of the hallway. "I need to go to the pharmacy tomorrow. They didn't have enough to fill my script, so I need to pick the rest up. The one in Benton Falls called here once I explained the situation I find myself in."

"I don't like it," I tell her. "I'll pick it up for you."

"You can't. They need my insurance card and for me to sign. After tomorrow you can go for me, but I'm new here, so I have to go."

I run my hands over my face because her going out in this shit is the last thing I want. Who knows what idiot drivers are going to be like with snow covered roads. They're bad enough when it's dry out. But, I'll give her this and make sure that I'm driving her. No one else is going to have my girl and my baby's life in their hands but me. That I won't allow to happen.

"Alright firefly. We'll go right after you eat breakfast."

She nods her head and I watch the girls surround her to find out what's going on. Whitney knows, and I see her hanging back. This is going to be a hard secret for her to keep, I can already tell. I can just imagine what Keegan is telling them to get them to back off for right now. I'll have to ask her when we're alone so that I know what she said if I'm asked.

"Firefly," I call out. "Come here babe."

Keegan walks over to me and I can tell the moment she starts to feel like she's going to be sick. So, I watch her sit down for a minute and let her body relax as much as possible. Whitney is heading her way and I'm trying to remain calm so no one else asks questions. I see Whitney block them so that she can discreetly hand her a few crackers to munch on. I nod over to Summer and she grabs a bottle of water to bring my girl.

Once I reach her, I kneel down so that I can get her what she needs. She just looks at me while she slowly eats her food and sips her water. Between Whitney and I, we're shielding her as much as we can. Looking over my shoulder, I can see the rest of the girls are waiting to get over here. Thankfully, their men are keeping them busy so that Keegan can do what she needs to do.

"You feelin' any better baby?" I ask her.

"Starting to. Thank you both," she says, relaxing even further back into the chair.

"Now, why did you get up to begin with firefly?" I ask, wanting to know what woke her up.

"Nothing really. I had to go to the bathroom and then I heard all the excitement out here. So, I decided to come see what was going on."

"Okay. Well, you want to help me put sweet pea to bed and then we'll go back to bed?"

"Yeah. I think that's the best idea,"

"Why don't you go get Kasey and I'll meet you in her room?" I ask, wanting to talk to Whitney for a second.

Keegan grabs my daughter and I watch them disappear down the hallway. Once I think that it's safe to talk, I sit down. This is going to be hard to ask because I don't know how to word it.

"Should she be like this?" I ask. "She's so tired all the time. It's like the littlest thing wears her out."

"I was tired in the beginning and the end. But, not like she is."

"Should I be more worried than I am right now?"

"Well, I think you need to talk to her doctor. She might have to do some tests or something."

"Fuck!" I call out, gaining unwanted attention.

"Don't get worked up. We'll take it a day at a time and see if she improves at all. Otherwise, you'll have to mention it to the doctor when she goes back. Rage, we'll all keep an eye on her, but I think you need to let people know so that they can help you. You're not going to be any good if you're worn down from worry and everything else."

"I'll talk to her. Now, I'm goin' to tuck my girl into bed with her and then get her back in bed."

Leaving Whitney, I take in what she's told me. I'll be keeping an eye on her and I think that we need to let the others know now too. At least those closest to us. Then, we can let everyone else know what's going on at another point in time. Hopefully she'll agree to that.

I walk into the room connected to mine and see Keegan kneeling down on the floor next to Kasey. My daughter is already in bed, covered up to her chin, with Keegan reading her a good night story to her. It's one of her princess stories that I've read countless times. Kasey has her favorites and I know that my girl has read this story to her while she's been at her house during the day.

Since I want to silently watch the interaction between my girl and daughter, I lean against the door frame, cross my arms over my chest, and cross my ankles. Keegan is reading the story and not paying attention to anything around her. I know I've made a noise or two while I was settling in, she hasn't looked up or paused in her story-telling. My sweet pea has her full attention and I love that more than anything. As I'm watching, I see Kasey's eyes starting to droop, so I know I don't have that much time before she's out for the night. Making my way in her room, I lean over Kasey and gently kiss her cheek as I check the blankets surrounding her.

As I'm making sure my daughter knows I was in here, Keegan doesn't miss a beat. She continues reading to Kasey. So, I sit behind her and pull her into my lap. My girl continues to read and is totally submersed into the story. She doesn't seem to realize anything that's going on around her. While she's safe in the clubhouse, I don't want to hear about her being like this when she's outside the walls.

"Firefly, I think she's asleep. Want to go to bed?" I ask her, lifting the book from her hands and setting on the stand by Kasey's bed.

"Yeah. Let's go babe."

Walking into our room, I watch my girl undress again before climbing into bed. She scoots over to the inside and waits for me to follow her. Keegan is looking up at me with wide eyes as I start undressing. I've finally gotten her to the point that she'll sleep naked next to me. Even though we had sex earlier, I'm ready to go again. I just don't want to push her and make her even sicker or anything like that.

"You keep watchin' me like that and you're gonna be in trouble," I tell her, stalking towards the bed.

"Maybe I want your kind of trouble," she answers, pulling the blankets back so I can climb in.

"Not tonight. Tonight, I'm goin' to hold you in my arms and we're goin' to sleep. We have a big day ahead of us."

"I can't wait. I want to have a snowball fight," she tells me, snuggling down in next to me.

"You sure about that firefly?" I ask, not liking the idea of her being involved in that.

"I am. A little snow isn't going to hurt me babe. If I get cold or anything else, I'll come back inside. I promise."

Keegan finally finishes burrowing into my side. Her arm wraps around me and she winds a leg between mine. This is how we normally sleep now. I love that she's comfortable enough to wrap her around me. However, I also know that as this pregnancy progresses, this won't be the way we're sleeping. So, I'm going to love it while I get it and wait patiently until I can have it back.

Keegan

This morning, waking up was the same as it has been. Getting up and rushing into the bathroom to get sick. Rage is instantly at my side and doing what he can to help me. Then, he hands me some ginger ale and crackers or dry toast. As soon as I know that I'm not going to get sick right away again, I take my medicine and wait for it to kick in.

"You get ready to go and I'll get Kasey her breakfast so she can hang here," Rage tells me.

"Okay babe."

I head back into the bathroom to complete my morning routine. Once I'm done, I head out in search of Rage and whoever else is going to be going with us today. I know that we're going to have an escort and make multiple stops. So, I make sure that I've packed up my crackers and a bottle of ginger ale.

Rage and Kasey are in the kitchen. She's eating eggs, toast, and bacon. The sight of the eggs makes me want to run to the bathroom, but I'm trying my hardest not to. Instead, I turn away from them and talk to Sami.

"How are you doing Sami?" I ask, sitting next to her.

"I'm okay. Trying to understand everything going on. But, I'm getting it. I think."

"What are you trying to understand?" I ask her, confused.

"How Goose acts here. He's a little different. I mean, he treats me the same way as he always does. But, the club girls are all over him."

"Oh honey," I begin. "I'm sorry you have to see that. But, it's a part of the life. Is he letting them make advances on him?"

"No. He makes sure that they know we're together. They give me evil looks and still try to tempt him to go be with them."

"Sami, he's not letting what they're doing get to him. So, watch and see what happens. As long as he stays true to you, you have nothing to worry about. And from what I've seen from the way he treats you, the way he watches you, and the way he looks at you, you have nothing to worry about. He is so in love with you," I tell her, making sure that she's truly hearing what I'm saying to her.

"I know he is. I just can't give him what they can. We're still going to wait until I turn eighteen to take our relationship to that level."

"If he wanted them, he wouldn't be with you. He'd be single, so he could be with them. Now, don't you think this is exactly what he was thinking when he told you to date boys your own age?"

"I know. And I love that he wanted to do that for me. But, I know that this is different."

"Not really. It's the same thing."

I leave Sami to sit and think about what we've talked about. She needs to make up her mind now whether or not she can handle Goose being around the club girls. I've seen him push them off of him whenever they try to push up on him. He's all about Sami and being with her. Sami needs to make her mind up one way or another before one of them gets hurt and it's not repairable.

Seeing that Kasey is done eating, I make my way over there. Rage pulls me in for a kiss and I can taste the coffee on his breath. It turns my stomach, but I can keep it under control. We'll have to talk about that later. He's telling Kasey that she needs to go in and get dressed for the day so she can spend it with Skylar and the rest of the kids. That gets her running down to her room, so she can get to the kids quicker.

"Are you ready to go firefly?" he asks me.

"Yeah. Just waiting on you sexy."

"Let me see who all is goin' and then we'll be off. I'll be right back," he tells me. "Do you have somethin' warm to wear?"

"Nope. The only time I needed a winter coat was when I lived with Riley. She has it now."

Rage stares at me for a minute and then shakes his head. Before heading towards Grim, he takes off down the hallway. I'm not sure what he's doing right now, so I take a seat on one of the couches. It's not long before Goose is joining me.

"I saw you talkin' to Sami earlier," he says.

"Yep."

"Everythin' good with her?"

"You need to talk to her. There's things you need to get out in the open. One of them being the club girls. Instead of sitting here with me, go find your girl and make sure she knows her place in your life."

Goose smiles at me before taking off in search of his girl. They are so cute together. Once they get their communication skills better, they'll make it just fine. The two of them have a love that's pure. She's still innocent in many ways and he wants to protect that with everything he is. At the same time, she wants to protect him and do what she has to do to make sure he's happy.

Finally, I see Rage walking back towards the common room. He's got something over his arm and I can't wait to see what it is. I'll have to wait though because he makes his way over to Grim first. There's a small group of men standing there and I'm sure that they're the ones that are going to be going with us on our outing.

"Firefly, come here," Rage says.

Making my way over there, he holds out a hoodie and another coat to me. I guess he's making sure that I'm going to be warm. I'm surprised he's not wrapping me in blankets and everything else to make sure I'm toasty warm and don't get cold at all. If I voice that thought aloud, I'm sure that will be his next step. So, we'll keep that to myself.

We all walk out to the SUV's and pile in. Rage is driving one and I notice that Wood and Boy Scout are with us. This is probably Rage's idea because they've been with me the last few weeks and he's seen the way they protect me. I'm thankful that it's them so if I do happen to get sick, I'm not going to have to explain it to anyone else riding with us. It's bad enough that Whitney knows. Which, I'm guessing means that Irish also knows.

"Where else are we going besides the pharmacy?" I ask.

"We have to go get shovels and winter clothes for everyone. There's not enough to go around, so Grim wants us to pick enough up for both clubs. Especially the kids. We all know it's just a matter of time before they want to head outside and play."

"Sounds good. Anything else we need?"

"Not right now. But, who knows if someone will call and give us a list of other things to get."

We've been out for hours now. Rage is getting frustrated because he doesn't want me out here still. But, Grim called with a list of groceries that we had to pick up. That was after scouring every stored in Clifton Falls for shovels, gloves, hats, coats, scarves, and a long list of other items. Two of the SUV's are already filled. Ours will be getting piled to the brim with groceries that we need.

As we're walking through the grocery store, I can't help but feeling like someone is watching us. I'm not sure that they're following us throughout the store, but I'm getting a little panicked. Rage can feel it, but he's not saying anything. He's following my cues and letting me tell him what's going on with me. I know this is only going to last so long before he starts demanding answers.

"Rage, I feel like we're being watched," I tell him finally.

"I figured that's what it was. I've been getting the feeling off and on too."

"Can we hurry up and head back to the clubhouse please?" I ask, wanting nothing more than to hurry up and get the hell out of here.

Rage is already typing away on his phone. I'm guessing that he's messaging the others to let them know that we're going to be getting out of here as quick as possible. He speeds up as we walk up and down the aisles, grabbing what we need for the clubhouse. We only make it down two aisles before Wood and Boy Scout are meeting us. Our carts are overflowing, and I know that we're going to need at least another cart once the groceries are put in bags. So, I go to make my way over to grab one until my man stops me. instead he sends Boy Scout over to get one.

As soon as we're done paying for everything, we make our way out to the SUV with four full carts. Wood realized that no one grabbed drinks and he ran back to get a cart filled with soda and drinks for the kids. He even managed to grab a few gallons of milk without any of us reminding him that we needed it. I'm not sure where all this food is going, but we'll make it fit somewhere in the amazing kitchen at the clubhouse.

"Firefly, get in the truck while we unload these carts please," Rage tells me.

I know he's worried as hell since we're both getting the feeling of being watched. He doesn't want anything to happen to me, so he's going to make sure that I'm sheltered and protected at all costs. Just as I go to get in the SUV, a car comes careening out of nowhere and just misses hitting the carts, the guys, and the SUV. I'm shocked and jarred from my position at the front door.

It's slippery out and I almost fall to the ground. Thankfully, Rage was close by and caught me before anything happened.

"What the fuck?" he yells out. "Where the fuck did that car come from?"

"I don't know man," Wood says, coming closer to us.

Before Rage can say another word, the rest of the guys that were with us are surrounding us. They didn't go in the store with us so that someone was out watching the SUV we're in. Rage told me that it was necessary in case Sam or my dad tried to do anything to it while no one was around. If they tried, they wouldn't know that anyone else was really watching it since the rest of the guys parked away from where we did.

"Did any of you see anythin'?" Wood asks as Rage is continuing to check me over.

"No. Before we saw anythin', the car was almost to you guys. The only thing that Killer said was that it looked like the person was lookin' for a parkin' space. I didn't see the car before you guys came out," Playboy tells the men.

"Where's Killer now?" Rage asks Playboy.

"He went to try to catch up with whoever just tried to hit you guys. We're gonna have packed SUV's. Killer isn't comin' back here. He's goin' to look for them and then head back to the clubhouse. Now, let's get this shit loaded up so that we can get on the road."

I climb in the passenger side door as the guys unload the carts. It doesn't take long with everyone working together so that we can get out of here and back to the safety of the clubhouse. I can feel the tension and anger radiating off the men riding with us. It's causing me to become even more panicked. This isn't going to be good for anyone involved. And, it's making me want to either run out and hide or use myself as bait to lure these assholes out in the open. The sooner this is done, the sooner everyone involved can get back to their normal lives.

However, I know that Rage and Whitney won't allow me to go out as bait. They'll want me to stay put and protect the baby and myself. I want to protect the baby with everything in me. The only way to do that is to end this shit with my dad and Sam. We'll never be safe until they're gone.

Walking back into the clubhouse, I see that there's more commotion going on. More than when it started to snow out. I can't help but wonder what's going on, until I see Grim come out of his office and look directly at me.

"Rage and firefly, need you to come here," he calls out. "Now!"

We look at one another and head towards his office. I can't think of any reason that he'd want to talk to us in his office. If it's regarding the situation at the store, I don't know why I'd be involved in this conversation. I'd assume it would be between the men of the club's. That way they could figure out if it was some random incident or something involving the asswipes after me.

"We got a situation and I don't know what to do about it," Grim tells us as he opens the door.

As soon as I walk through the door, my eyes almost pop out of my head. Sitting in front of Grim's desk is Riley. I never thought I'd see her again and now that she's here, I need to know what's going on with her. If she's in trouble, we need to know. Or, did my dad and

Sam find her and get their hooks in her? Is she here on behalf of them? I can't help but be suspicious of her motives and I've never done that before.

"Riley!" I call, and she turns her head towards me. "What are you doing here?"

"Keegan! You're really here? They didn't find you?" she asks, tears streaming down her cheeks.

"No, they don't have me. What's going on? Why are you here?" I ask, letting the concern and suspicion come out full force.

"I had to find you. I got a letter in the mail from your dad. He said that they found you and were in the process of taking you from the men who kidnapped you. This man here, has been trying to tell me you're not kidnapped. That you're here of your own free will."

"I'm not kidnapped," I tell her, not understanding what's going on still.

"Who the fuck sent you here?" Rage bellows out. He's not holding his anger back.

"N-n-no one sent me here. I came to check on my best friend. This man has kept me in his office until you guys got back. Can I spend time with her please?"

"Not until I know that you're not lyin' to us. I'm protectin' my girl at all costs. Even from you!" he tells her, and I burrow into him further for his loving ways.

"Why would I lie? I have nothing to gain by causing her harm. Keegan, you know I love you and I don't want them to find you. Please, tell them that," Riley pleads with me.

"I really want to believe you Riley. I'm so hurt right now at my doubt. But, after today and the letters that I've been getting, I can't trust anyone. I need to know that they haven't gotten to you," I tell her, not being able to hold back my emotions any longer.

"I know you're trying to protect yourself. You'll see that I'm telling you the truth," Riley tells me standing up.

Before anyone can react, she's whipping her shirt off and standing before us with nothing more than bandages covering her. I want to tell her to stop, not to show us what's under those bandages, but I know it's useless. Riley makes sure to keep herself covered as much as she can, but, pulling the bandages off, I begin to see three words carved into her once flawless skin. The first word is 'Whore', the second one is 'Liar', and the third word is 'Traitor.'

"I don't understand why you have the word traitor carved into you," I begin, too confused to comprehend what it means.

"Sam got to me before I met you. He knew you'd be coming through my town. I was supposed to meet you, get to know you, and then make sure you stayed where you were. Sam was going to come get you from me," Riley begins. "As soon as I met you though, I couldn't go through with it. There was no way I was going to hand you over to that animal."

I stand there, and shock takes over. There's no way that Riley was working for Sam. What the fuck? Everything I've ever thought about my friendship with her is now being brought into question. Was anything she ever said to me true? Could she really be working for them still? Is there any way that she's going to be truthful now? I don't know what I'm supposed to do now. On one hand, I want to trust in Riley and protect her. On the other hand, I don't know if I can ever trust her again.

"Firefly, are you okay?" Rage asks me. "I don't know what to do here."

"I don't know. Riley, I wish I could trust you still. Right now, I need to think about everything and I'll let you know as soon as I figure it out."

"I get it," she tells me. "Please know that I got these marks I'll have for the rest of my life because I refused to give you up to those animals. When I first agreed, I wasn't in a good place. You know what I've been through. As soon as I took one look at you, I knew that Sam was lying to me. That's why I couldn't turn you over to them. You became my best friend and the sister I never had. Trust in that Keegan."

There's no way that I can stay in here any longer. Taking one more look at Riley, I see the tears falling down her cheeks and the agony running through her. I look up to my man and let him know without words that I want her kept here, but that I need some time and space. Heading out to the common room, I look at all the controlled chaos going on to get everything put away and keep everyone organized while the men start cleaning up the snow. It's still falling, but at a much slower rate.

"Are you okay?" Whitney asks me, appearing out of nowhere.

"I don't know right now. Everything I thought I knew about Riley was a lie. Right now, I want to believe her, but I can't."

"I know you're upset, but was everything really a lie when she got carved up like me? And, she is here now, telling you all the truth," Whitney begins. "I'm sure the guys will get the rest of the story from her. But, she's here now wanting to make sure that you're okay and weren't kidnapped like she was led to believe."

I nod to my cousin to make sure she knows that I'm listening to what she's saying. Right now, I just need some alone time. It's going to take time to process not only what Riley dropped on me, but what Whitney told me too. As usual, my cousin makes sense. I'm just so heartbroken that my friendship for the first time in my life started out as a lie. A way for Riley to get out of trouble and to possibly hand me over to the men that I was running from in the first place.

While Rage is still in the office, I make my way to the room we're staying in. I need to put my medicine up so that I can go help everyone get things done. There's groceries to be put away, snow gear to organize, and Kasey wanted to play outside. She was adamant that we were going to have a snowball fight. So, I wasn't going to disappoint her. If that's what she wanted to do, then that's what we were going to do. It would probably help take my mind off everything with Riley too.

We've been working for what seems like hours. Everything is finally put away and the men have been out working on clearing away the snow. Skylar has been in the kitchen non-stop making hot cocoa and coffee for the men as they come in to warm up. I've been in and out helping her. Everyone has a job to do and we all do it without complaint or too much chaos.

During the entire time, my mind keeps drifting back to Riley. I want to go see her, but I know that now isn't the time to do that. I'm still too confused and I want to talk to Rage before I go in there with her. The only thing I've heard is that they've put her in a room by herself and one of the prospects is standing guard. Tank's the one that told me that. I think he wanted to make sure that I had some sort of peace of mind as I went about my day.

"Keegan!" Kasey hollers, running up to me. "Keegan!"

"What's up sweet pea?" I ask, using Rage's nickname for her.

Kasey giggles at my use of it. I love hearing her little girl giggle and I try my hardest to hear it every day I'm with her. It reminds me of when Whitney and I were younger and carefree. We used to laugh and play with no regard for the things we would soon have to deal with because of our dad's.

"It's almost time for our snowball fight. Daddy said that I need to get warmer clothes on and then we'll be heading out. Are you coming with us?" Kasey asks, excitement making her words almost run into one another. I'm surprised she got it all out in one breath.

"Is that right? Are you sure you want me to go out with you? I mean, I might throw like a girl," I tell her, trying to make her giggle again.

"It's okay if you throw like a girl. We'll just get really close to daddy, so we hit him," she whispers loudly to me.

Out of the corner of my eye, I see Rage standing there. He's trying his hardest not to laugh at his daughter. I can tell that he doesn't want her to know that he overheard her plan to get close to him and attack. Currently, he's leaning against the wall, his ankles crossed, holding clothes for Kasey to bundle up in. The man always looks sexy as fuck, but when he's with is daughter or doing something for her, he's at his sexiest. Kasey becomes his entire center and nothing, and no one, else matters to him.

"Well, then I think we should go get ready to go outside then. What about you?"

"Yay!" Kasey hollers and spins to go in search of her dad.

I watch as Kasey squirms and continues moving while Rage tries to dress her in warm clothes. When we were shopping, I picked her out a coat, snow pants, a hat, gloves, and a scarf. They're in pinks and purples which are her favorite colors. Her eyes popped out and the smile that graced her face was a moment that I'll always treasure. It was like we gave her the world instead of clothes to stay warm.

In the meantime, I put my own jacket and gloves on. I forgot to get myself a hat while we were out, so I'll have to wear a hoodie and hope that I stay warm enough. Otherwise, I already know that Rage won't let me stay outside for long. Hell, I'm surprised that he's letting me out to play at all.

"Firefly, we're ready," Rage tells me, coming up to me. "Are you ready to go?"

"Yeah."

"Where's your hat?" he asks.

"I forgot to get one," I answer honestly.

My man takes the hat off his head and places it on mine. Then he pulls the hood of his hoodie up like I was going to do. Once he makes sure that we're all dressed warm, he leads us outside. I'm surprised at how many others are already out here. It looks like we're getting separated into teams. Kasey and I end up on the same team while Rage ends up with most of the guys.

We all start making snowballs before the actual fight begins. I'm helping Kasey and stockpiling as many as I can. I see Jameson is helping Zoey and sticking close to her. Even while he's doing that, he's still watching all the kids. Most of the little boys are doing the same thing. It's cute to watch them go all protective like the men of the club.

"Alright, is everyone ready?" Slim calls out.

Everyone screams their response before Slim does a countdown. Kasey is trying to sneak up closer to Rage while the rest of us are paying attention to the countdown. All of the adults are trying to contain their laughter at her antics. Especially since Rage is acting like he doesn't see her approaching him. I fall in love with this man more every day.

We're all poised to start launching snowballs at one another. Kasey, in all her excitement, wants to gain an edge on her daddy so bad that she lets her snowball fly early and hit's him right in the stomach. He pretends that he was mortally wounded while we all laugh hysterically at their antics. This is what we needed today. What I needed to distract me from all thoughts of Riley and the mess she just brought here.

"Daddy! I got you!" Kasey yells out.

"Yes, you did sweet pea," Rage answers. "Now, I'm gonna get you?"

"No! Daddy, no!" Kasey screams out, running to hide behind me.

I can see the sparkle in Rage's eyes as he plays with his daughter. To him, it doesn't matter that there's a crowd around them. The club members and anyone else around are a witness at any given moment to the love and laughter Rage and Kasey share. This is how it should be between a dad and his daughter. There should always be laughter, love, and the feeling of being safe. When it comes to the two that hold my heart, there is no doubt to anyone in the world that Kasey is loved and everything else that she needs.

As I'm standing here daydreaming, the snowball fight is going on around me. I guess I better get my head in the game, before I end up getting hit and Rage gets pissed. Just as I go to take aim at my man, my stomach revolts and I need to run inside. This is not good. But, I should've known it was bound to happen. We've been having fun and I didn't really eat lunch today. So, I take off towards the bathroom. Rage is behind me, I can hear him calling for me, but I can't slow down. If I do, I won't make it.

Once I'm done in the bathroom, we walk out to see all the girls in the hallway. They're waiting for me and I know that my time to keep this secret has run out. The only thing I want to do is go take a nap, but if I've learned anything since being around the club, it's that these girls won't stop until you let them know what they want to know.

"Alright, we know that Whitney knows what's going on with you," Bailey starts. "We're a group of old ladies and we stick together. So, now, someone is going to fill the rest of us in on what's going on with you Keegan."

I look back to Rage and see him nod his head at me. He knows that this is what I have to do. In fact, I'm sure it was only a matter of time before he came to me about telling certain people. It's just a matter of being scared because I was beaten to the point I had a miscarriage before. I don't want anything to happen to this baby.

"Let's go in the kitchen and I'll make us some hot cocoa," Skylar begins. "Then you can tell us what's going on. Fill us in on the story that you want to hide. We'll figure it out honey."

Rage leaves me to go with the rest of the girls. I'm sure that he's going to make his way back out to Kasey and the snowball fight. He'll make sure that she's distracted while we're talking. This is going to hurt her since we told her that she could be the one to break the news about the baby. I'll let them know so that they can act surprised when we make the announcement.

As Skylar's working on making hot cocoa for everyone, the rest of us sit down and get comfortable. I want to wait until she's over here, but from the looks I'm getting, I don't think that's going to be possible.

"We know why you left," Maddie begins. "Now, we want to know what's happened since you've been gone. There hasn't been time to catch up properly."

"Well, I found out when I was in Benton Falls that I am pregnant," I tell them.

The girls sit there in stunned silence for a few minutes. I'm not sure what they're waiting for, but the looks on their faces are pretty comical. They range from stun, surprise, shock, and understanding. Finally, Skylar lets out a squeal of happiness and runs over to hug me. The rest of them quickly follow suit and I'm engulfed in them all trying to hug me at the same time. At least until we hear someone clearing their throat from the doorway.

"Everythin' okay in here?" Irish asks, walking up to Whitney.

"More than okay," Bailey answers, she looks at me silently asking if we can let him know.

I shake my head so that he is kept in the dark. Kasey needs to be the one to break the news to everyone else. We promised her that and I'm going to make sure we keep that promise. Bailey respects my wishes and quickly ushers Irish out of the kitchen. I'm guessing that everyone is going to be heading back inside, so maybe I should talk to Rage about making the announcement.

Making my excuses, I make my way out to find my man and Kasey. As long as we're all going to be here, we might as well tell everyone now what's going on. I'm sure that Kasey has been waiting and waiting to be able to let everyone know she's going to be a big sister. I find them sitting at a table with Grim and Glock. Once Rage sees me, he looks to make sure I'm okay. I nod my head to let him know I'm good.

"I think it's time," I tell him, sitting down between him and Glock.

"Are you sure?"

"Yeah. Let her have her moment now. People are starting to wonder and we're not going to be able to hide it much longer."

"Sweet pea, are you ready to share our news?" Rage asks Kasey.

"Yes!" she yells out excitedly.

Rage walks Kasey over to the bar and stands her on top of it. He gets everyone's attention and waits until the common room goes deadly silent. Whispering to his daughter, I see the excitement shining from her eyes.

"We gots some news!" Kasey begins, talking loudly and excitedly. "I'm gonna be a big sister! My Keegan's gonna have a baby!"

There's no movement or noise in the clubhouse for a minute. Finally, everyone starts talking and congratulating us all at once. It's chaos at it's best and I'm so glad that I'm back with the people that are truly my family. These people have made me the happiest I've ever been, and I will never be able to thank them for accepting me into their fold with no questions asked. Other than what I was running and hiding from.

Rage brings Kasey down from the bar top and she hugs us both. It's been her and her dad for so long that she's can't wait to meet the new baby. We've had talks about it. There's a whole list of things that she already wants to do with the baby. And, she keeps telling me that she's even going to help change the dirty, stinky diapers.

"You happy soon to be mama?" Rage asks, pulling me into his side.

"I am. What more could we ask for? We've got friends by our side, family, playing out in the snow, and the holidays are fast approaching," I tell him, snuggling in even closer.

"I could think of a few things."

"Like what?" I ask, wanting to know what he's talking about.

"Well, for starters, your dad and that asswipe bein' out of the equation. Then, havin' a home of our own."

"You want to have a house with me?" I ask astonished. I mean I didn't think we'd stay at the clubhouse permanently. But, I didn't think he'd want to get a house with me already.

"Of course. I've already started it. See, I listen when you talk firefly. I know what you want and what you don't want."

"Are you serious? When can I see it?" I ask, the excitement building the more I think about sharing a home with this family.

"I'll see what kind of progress gets made this week and then I'll show it to you. Right now, it's not much to look at."

Without hesitation, I reach up and pull Rage down to meet my lips. Before it can get too heated, I hear a muffled 'ew' coming from Kasey. This leads to everyone surrounding us laughing like crazy. Yeah, we might have forgotten we had an audience.

"We'll continue this later on. After Kasey has gone to bed," Rage tells me, slapping my ass before walking over to join some of the guys.

Chapter Four

Keegan

I CAN'T BELIEVE HOW FAST TIME is flying by. We've been playing in the snow, spending time with everyone in the clubhouse, and now we're planning for Thanksgiving in a few weeks. I'm excited because it will be my first celebration with family. In the month that's gone by, every single one of these individuals have become my family.

At the same time, I'm trying to slowly ease back into spending time with Riley. Things aren't the same as it used to be, and honestly, I don't know that they ever will be again. She's been trying to tell me what exactly happened and what made her change her mind. While I appreciate that she's trying to be honest now, I think she should've been honest from the very beginning. We could have come up with a game plan back then.

Today, I have to take time away from helping the rest of the girls plan for Thanksgiving. Rage and I are going to see Doctor Sanchez. He's really concerned about how tired I am and the way that I'm still getting sick. Honestly, I am too. Bailey and the rest of the girls have talked to me about this and they've all told me that they think I'm carrying multiples. They just aren't sure if it's twins or more. That thought scares the ever-loving shit out of me honestly.

"Are you almost ready firefly?" Rage asks, coming in our room.

"Yeah. I just need to brush my hair and we'll be ready to head out."

"I'll be in the truck waitin'. I'm just gonna drop Kasey off in the game room with the girls."

Rage gives me a kiss and then walks out of the room. It's probably a good thing because I'm distracted to the point that I'm forgetting things this morning. I went to take a shower, and I forgot all my clothes in the room. Thankfully, I locked the door before I got in, so I didn't have to worry about anyone walking in. But, first I forgot that I was making Kasey eggs and toast this morning and completely burned everything. It was insane. We had to open all the windows and doors to get the horrid smell out of the clubhouse.

It doesn't take me long to get done brushing my hair. So, I grab my purse and head out to the truck. Rage bought one a week ago. He decided that we needed something better for the winter months. Especially with the baby on the way. The car that I've been driving is good enough with the three of us, but not now that there's at least one more baby on the way. I haven't even told him about the possibility of there being more than one baby in there.

On our way to the doctor's office, he holds my hand. I'm not sure if he's trying to calm me down or calm himself down. I know he's been worried about how sick and tired I've been. It's something that we're going to talk to the doctor about today. Rage and I talked about it last night and I agreed that we need to find out what's going on.

Today is the first time that I'm walking into a doctor's office with Rage. He doesn't let me go to the counter alone or anything. The entire time, he's right by my side. Especially when I finally got called back to go in the exam room. I'm not going to do a single thing alone during this pregnancy. It's refreshing to know that I'm not going to be alone.

"How has everything been going?" the nurse asks me.

"I've still been really sick and I'm sleeping a lot. I know I've heard that you get tired in the beginning of your pregnancy, but the way I sleep is insane. It's all I want to do."

"Well, we can do some blood work and an ultrasound. Then we can try to figure out what's going on and what we need to do next," Doctor Sanchez tells me.

"Sounds good," Rage answers.

As soon as I got on the exam table, he pulled the chair up by my head and hasn't moved from that spot since. He's not going to be going too far from me if he doesn't have to. Honestly, I didn't think I was going to like the attention, I figured I'd feel suffocated. The opposite is actually true. I feel so loved and wanted, like he's true when he tells me that he's going to be by my side and protect me, and our family, no matter what.

Doctor Sanchez does what she has to do as far as my exam goes. Once she's done, she makes the arrangements for me to have an ultrasound done. She wants it done today with the way that I'm feeling. Having a doctor that is going to go above and beyond to make sure that I'm okay is amazing. I've heard horror stories where the patient could barely get a word in about something that was going on. I don't know what I'd do if I ended up with someone like that.

"Okay, stay right here," she tells us coming back in the room. "The technician will be here shortly. On your way out, make sure that you make an appointment for another month from now."

We thank the doctor before she leaves the room. Once again, she makes sure that I have the medicine I need to stop feeling so nauseous. It helps a little bit, but I can't constantly take it, so there's going to be times that I'm going to have to deal with it.

"Are you excited to see the baby?" I ask Rage.

"Yeah. I know it's not goin' to look like much since you aren't that far along, but it's better than nothin'," he answers.

I can see the excitement in his eyes. It makes me wonder if he got to go through anything when his ex was pregnant with Kasey. If he didn't, my heart breaks for him. Rage is such an amazing man and a wonderful father. Our little boy or girl is going to be so loved and cherished. This pregnancy also makes me realize that I wasn't anywhere near ready to have a baby when I was pregnant before. I'm glad that I get to experience this with the man at my side and not someone else.

"Can I ask you something without upsetting you?" I ask him hesitantly.

"Of course, you can. Don't ever be afraid to ask me anythin' firefly."

"Did you get to go through this with Kasey's mom? Were you still together when she was pregnant?"

"No. She wouldn't let me around her. I got told she was pregnant through a text message. Once in a while I'd get an update, but that's it. Hell, I was barely there when Kasey was born. If it wasn't for my mom, I wouldn't have known at all."

"I'm so sorry," I tell him, my heart breaking.

"Nothin' to be sorry about. It's in the past and I have Kasey all to myself now. Plus, I get to experience it with you now."

"I would never hold this from you. No matter what happens between us, I'd never have kept your baby from you."

"I know firefly."

Before anything else can be said, there's a knock on the door and it's opened. There's a technician wheeling a big machine in behind her. I'm not sure exactly what I'm supposed to be seeing here, but I'm sure she knows exactly what she's doing. Rage has a confused expression on his face too. We look at one another and I know that we're both clueless in this moment.

"How are you today?" the tech asks.

"We're doing good," I answer, noticing that she's not looking in my man's direction at all.

"Okay. This is going to be an internal ultrasound. Have you heard of that before?"

"No."

The technician explains what's going to happen. I watch as Rage's face pales. If I wasn't so worried about what's going on, I'd laugh at him. But, this is to make sure that our baby is fine, so I just grab his hand and hold on tight. This makes Rage look at me and I know he can see the concern I have for him. So, he leans over and kisses me gently while she gets everything ready.

Once she's ready to go, she tells me to push my pants down. Once I have them removed, she does what she has to do so we can see our baby on the screen. The only reason I know this is because she told us that's what was going to happen. Within a minute there's a picture up on the screen and I'm staring at it in fascination. Even though I have no clue what I'm looking at, I know that our child is in there. A child that was created out of love.

She points out different things and then my man asks the question that was in my head. "Um, why does it look like there are two tiny blobs in there?"

"That would be because there are two in there. It looks like you'll be having twins," the technician tells us.

I glance over at Rage and he's staring at me with love shining from him. I'm not sure what's going through his head right now though. Personally, I'm scared shitless knowing that we're going to be bringing two little ones into this world. Our family is getting bigger than we anticipated, but I know that with him by my side, we'll be more than fine. Rage isn't going to be an absent dad that expects me to do it all on my own. He'll be there for the midnight feedings, the dirty diapers, the crying, the first moments such as their first smile, walking, crawling, and talking. We're going to go through the hard times and the good times as a unit.

As we're walking back in the clubhouse, Rage is staring at the pictures from the ultrasound. He's been so quiet on the way here and I don't know how to take it. I'm sure he's surprised just like I am, but him not saying a single word is unnerving. If I weren't just as shocked, I would probably be upset right now.

"Are you okay?" I finally ask him.

"Yeah. I'm shocked, surprised, happy as fuck, and scared," he tells me, wrapping his arms around me and pulling me in for a delicious kiss.

"Should we tell Kasey?"

"Yeah. Let's find her and let her know. Then she'll let everyone else know."

That's another thing that I'm so happy about. We are including her in every part of this. We're not excluding her or making her feel like we're trying to replace her or anything. Kasey will be a part of this every step of the way. It's the only way that she's not going to feel anything bad about it. And, if we're going to be a family, I want her included in everything. I already love her so much and feel like she's my daughter.

"Keegan! Daddy!" we hear shouted from the hallway. "You're back!"

Kasey comes running up to us and if we didn't know, we'd have missed catching her as she threw herself into our arms. This is what she always does though, so we were both ready. After hugging her and placing kisses all over her little angelic face, we tell her that we have some news for her. Rage walks us over to a table in the corner, so we can share this privately.

"Do you want to see somethin' amazin'?" he asks her, holding the pictures close to him.

"Yeah!" she says, bouncing in her seat.

"These are pictures of the babies growing in Keegan's belly," he tells her, placing the pictures on the table in front of her.

"Why is there two Keegan?" she asks, looking up at me.

"Well, that's because we're going to be having two babies," I tell her, waiting to hear what she's going to say to that.

After pausing to think about it for a minute, a smile breaks out on her face. "You mean I get to be a big sister to two new babies? At the same time?"

"Yes, sweet pea," her dad answers her.

"This is so exciting! Can I tell? Please daddy? Please Keegan?" she begs us.

"You can. Wait until dinner when there's more people here. Can you do that honey?" Rage asks.

"I can daddy!"

Kasey gets up, hugs, and kisses us both before pausing in front of me. She's staring at my stomach, so I spread my arms wide. As soon as she has room, Kasey leans in and presses two little kisses to my stomach. Looking at Rage, I have tears glistening in my eyes at the sweetness coming from this amazing little girl standing before me.

Rage

Hearing that we're having twins was definitely a shock to the system. That was honestly the last thing I was expecting to hear today. I'm honestly excited at the aspect of having two new additions to our family. No matter what anyone says, we are a family. Right now, we're a family of three, soon we're going to be a family of five. And then, we'll be a bigger family eventually.

After Kasey, I never really thought about having more kids. Once I knew that I wanted Keegan in my life as something more than a quick fuck, I knew that I wanted her to have my babies. As many as she'll give me. I want to watch her grow round with baby's that we created from love and passion.

I know that we haven't said that we love one another, I don't want to scare her away. But, I know deep in my heart that I love Keegan. She loves me too, even if she hasn't said it. Firefly shows me every day that it's true. It's in the little things she does, the way she treats my daughter, and the way that she is with my brothers and old ladies in the club.

"Rage, I want to tell you something," she suddenly says, breaking me from the thoughts going around my mind.

"What's up firefly?" I ask, hoping that everything is okay.

"I know it's soon, but I can't hold it in. The time that I spent away from you and Kasey proved to me what I already knew before I took off," she begins, playing with the hem of her shirt. This is a sure sign that she's nervous. "I love Kasey and you. You two have become my entire world and I don't know what I'll do if anything ever happens to either one of you. It's soon, and I'm sorry for springing this on you, but I need to say it. These two new babies were created with the love we share. You don't have to say anything….."

I cut my girl off by placing my finger over her delectable lips. There's no way I can allow her to think that I don't feel the same way about her. If she honestly feels like I don't share her love, then I need to step up my game and make sure there's never a doubt in her mind.

"Firefly, I love you. At the current moment, there are four people I would lay down my life for with no second thoughts. That's Kasey, you, and the two new baby's you're carryin'. Eventually, we'll have more kids. I don't want anyone other than you. In the short amount of time we've known one another, you have become as important as Kasey to me. You guys are my entire world and if I were to lose either one of you, there wouldn't be anyone stoppin' me from goin' off the rails. I would destroy anyone that hurt you, and anyone that got in my way. I love you and one day I'm goin' to marry you."

Keegan has tears in her eyes, something that happens a lot these days. She gets up from her chair and makes her way over to me. So, I push my chair back and allow her to straddle my lap. This is not the time to be starting anything, but my cock has other ideas as it grows painfully hard underneath Keegan. Firefly starts placing little kisses all over my face until she makes her way to my neck. Once there, it's all over. I need my girl now and we need to get to our room. Hopefully I can make it there.

I carry Keegan to our room and slam the door shut behind us. Making my way over to the bed, I gently lay her down so that I can undress her as I worship her body. No matter how hard or fast I want to take her right now, I need to show her how much I truly love her. So, I'll let her know through our bodies. Words will only do so much to convince her of the love I feel for her.

As soon as I have my girl naked and laying in the middle of the bed, I take a minute to stare down at all that belongs to me. Keegan is squirming on the bed under my heated gaze. Her hair is fanned out behind her and the love she feels is radiating from her entire body. Finally, I can't take it anymore and I get naked as quickly as I possibly can.

Crawling up the bed between her silky thighs, I kiss, lick, and nip every inch of her. This only serves to make my girl squirm and pant even more. Reaching my destination, I take a minute to look at my pussy. Just as I go to take my first taste of the day, I look up in Keegan's eyes so she can see everything I'm feeling in this moment. As my tongue swipes through her folds on my way to her clit, Keegan gasps and arches up off the bed. She is so responsive to my touch and has no problem letting me know what she likes, what she doesn't, and what she needs. Perfection is laying under me.

As I pay close attention to her clit, I slide two fingers in her. Her greedy pussy is trying to suck them in and not let me pull them back out. We've just started and she's already so close to cumming. It amazes me sometimes that I am lucky enough to have this girl in my life. Keegan is panting and moaning as I continue to work her over, getting her ready to take me.

When I can't stand it anymore, I make my way up her body. Keegan is so close to finding her release, but it's not going to be by my tongue and fingers. I stop and pay special attention to her tit's. She's always been sensitive there and it's only gotten worse since she got pregnant.

"I love you firefly," I tell her as I slide inside where my cock loves to be.

"I love you," she pants out.

I slowly slide in and out of her, keeping my gaze on her. We stare at one another and there's no doubt about the love we both feel. This moment is ours. Keegan starts to meet every thrust. She's getting so close and I know that it's only a matter of time before I feel her clench around me, trying to draw every last drop from me.

Leaning up, Keegan starts to kiss my neck and chest. She's running her fingers through my hair and I love the feelings she's creating in me. Every little sensation she makes me feel is magnified this time. I'm not sure if it's because we declared our love for one another or if it's because of everything that we're going through right now. I'm not going to question it though.

"So. Close," she pants out.

"Give it to me," I growl out.

Keegan reaches down between us and starts frantically rubbing on her clit. She's pinching it and pulling it as much as she can. Knowing that Keegan has no problems making sure that she reaches her release turns me on like nothing else. Especially knowing that she's going to do what she has to do to make sure that I enjoy myself and find mine too.

"Aiden!" she screams out as her body arches off the bed.

I feel her muscles squeezing me and I know that I'm not going to last any longer. "Keegan!" I growl out.

As we both come down from one of the best orgasms I've ever had, I roll us onto our sides and don't let go. These are some of the best moments with my girl. She's satisfied, happy, and laying in my arms. We run our hands up and down one another in a loving way as our breath slows down. Keegan is looking up at me as she cups my cheek, letting every single emotion flood from her into me. I'm so glad that I found the love of my life. I'll spend every day I'm alive cherishing her and making her feel what I feel for her.

"I love you so much firefly," I tell her, placing a kiss at her temple.

"I love you more than you know," she tells me right back.

Dinner time has finally arrived, and Kasey is bouncing around the clubhouse. Everyone is trying to get it out of her what she's so excited about. Kasey is keeping her lips sealed about our secret though. She knows when it's time to let everyone in on it.

"Daddy, is it time?" she asks, running up to me as I'm making her a plate.

"It's time," I tell her, looking around to see most everyone already eating.

So, I place her back up on the bar while Keegan comes up to stand with us. I pull her in close and keep my arm wrapped around her. My other hand is on my daughter so that she doesn't fall in all of her excitement. Once I know we're ready, I whistle to get everyone's attention. Kasey is looking to make sure everyone is looking at her.

"Keegan and daddy are gonna have two babies!" she shouts out, making sure to accentuate 'two'. "I get two little babies to love!"

Once again, everyone starts cheering and coming up to congratulate us. Keegan and I are brimming with happiness, and I know moments like these are few and far between in our world. Our family is surrounding us as we get to celebrate adding to our family. For now, the threat of her dad and Sam are forced to the back of our minds. Having twins and celebrating is the only thing we're thinking about right now. I wish we would've taken a little longer to be surrounded by our family and loved one. However, you really don't know what's going to happen at any given second.

Chapter Five

Keegan

THE LAST FEW WEEKS HAVE FLOWN by. We've been preparing for Thanksgiving and going out shopping for Black Friday. Rage isn't happy about me going, but Pops and Alice are taking the kids so that we can all go. As long as I have my man by my side, nothing will happen to me. He'll make sure I'm protected at all costs.

It's the day before Thanksgiving and we're all in the kitchen baking, laughing, and having a great time. Skylar is making sure that everything is going according to some insane schedule that she has. It's funny to see the usually sweet and calm girl barking out orders and being demanding. Bailey can't help but tease her about it.

"I didn't know we were working with my brother today," Bailey says, passing by Skylar to get more flour.

"Very funny!" Skylar replies. "This is the first holiday I'm baking for with more than one club present. I want everything perfect."

"It's not like my dad's club hasn't had your food before. They know what you can do," Maddie reassures her.

"I know. I'm putting more pressure on myself than what I need to. It's just me and I'm sorry I'm driving you all crazy," she tells us all, making sure we know that she's sincere.

"It's not a big deal," Sami says. "We all still love you and we'll deal with your crazy because you deal with all of us when we go a little bit crazy."

Sami says just what's needed to break any remaining tension between us. I think I'm the only one that was feeling it because I'm the newest member of this crazy group of loveable women. I can't wait to see what happens when we go shopping. From what I hear, there's going to be trouble. They filled me in on the dressing room incident with Wood almost getting his ass handed to him because he saw Darcy and the rest of the girls in lingerie. This man seems to get the raw end of the deal constantly.

We continue working until Skylar decides that enough desserts are made. We've also made any of the food that we can before she starts the main courses tomorrow. Knowing that I'm not needed any longer in the kitchen, I make my way out back. The kids are out there playing and it's the kind of peacefulness that I need right now.

I find a seat close to the play area, but far enough away to let them have their privacy and continue playing their games. Jameson is playing with Zoey. He's trying to teach her something from the looks of it. Already she's looking at him with adoration in her eyes. I can see her idolizing him and I can guarantee that soon that will turn into a crush on him.

There's so many kids out here and I can't wait to add to the mix. Honestly, I think the only child not out here is Melody's baby. Lacie's not quite one and Melody still keeps her pretty close. I'm still nervous and scared as hell to be having twins, but I know that we'll be more than fine. If we have any questions, there's people here to help us out and make sure that we're good. Hell, Skylar has three sets of twins, so she's probably going to be my go to person when I have a question. I'm sure she'll get sick of me before too long with the questions I'm going to ask her.

"What are you doin' out here?" Rage asks, sitting beside me.

"I just needed a minute. And what better place to sit than where all the kids are. Are you really happy that we're having twins?" I ask, almost not wanting to hear his answer.

"Firefly, we could be havin' twins, triplets, one baby, it really doesn't matter to me. As long as they're healthy I'm good."

I pull my man close and kiss him sweetly. There's not much we can do with all of the kids running around. And, there's two prospects out here keeping an eye on them. I think they'll have a run for their money though the way Jameson and Anthony are keeping an eye on everything. I've heard the stories about them, but this is really the first time I'm seeing it firsthand.

"If you're happy, then I'm happy," I tell him.

I'd be happy either way, but knowing that he's happy with our surprise makes it that much better. Kasey is over the moon at the prospect of having two little babies added to our family. With all of the excitement around me, I can't help but join in. It's becoming more than my nerves or being scared. At least we know why I've been so tired lately. Skylar and Maddie both said they felt the same way when they were pregnant. For now, though, I'm content to sit with my man and watch our extended family love one another and watch the kids enjoy themselves without a care in the world.

It's been a hectic few days. Today, we're back in the kitchen making Thanksgiving dinner. Skylar isn't being as bossy as she was yesterday. Instead, we're all laughing, having fun, and enjoying spending the time together. The men are moving tables around in the common room, so we can get as many of us at one table as possible. It shouldn't be too hard considering the kids wanted their own little table to eat. They didn't want to be with the 'boring' adults.

"How are you feeling today?" Sami asks me.

"I'm tired, but a little better than before. I don't get sick quite as often."

"It's a good thing with all this food and the amazing smells going on right now," Melody tells me.

"I know. Thankfully, it's almost done and we can eat soon," I say, staring at all of the food.

The girls laugh at me, knowing that I'm probably going to get a huge plate and then eat a few bites. It's what I've been doing lately, but I get food in my stomach so that's all that matters. Well, unless your Rage. He thinks I need to be eating more than what I am right now. When he makes a plate for me, it's like he's feeding three of the men at one time. It's comical really the way he wants me to eat.

"The turkey should be done in a few hours. So, now we wait until it's time to turn everything else on. It's all ready to go, we just can't do anything with it yet," Skylar informs us all. "I don't know about you guys, but I'm going to get some rest."

"Is that what they're calling it now?" Bailey asks, making us all laugh.

"Very funny!"

We all make our way out of the kitchen. I see Rage and Kasey sitting in the main room. I'm not sure what they're doing, but I make my way over to them. The closer I get to them, they stop talking and both look up at me. This makes me kind of suspicious there's nothing I can do about it though. I wouldn't have the first idea what they'd be talking about that I can't hear.

"So, what are you doin' now firefly?" Rage asks, pulling me in for a kiss.

"I actually think I'm going to go lay down for a little bit. I'm tired and I need to be rested for our plans later tonight."

"Okay. Well, Kasey and I have a few things to do, so we'll see you later on. I love you firefly," he tells me, sitting me in his lap.

For a minute I can't say anything. This is the first time that he's told me he loves me in front of anyone else and I'm shocked speechless. Don't get me wrong, I do love this man with everything in me. Looking at Rage, I can see how unsure he is right now. I need to tell him how I feel, but the words are stuck in my throat as tears form in my eyes.

"Um….Just forget," he begins to say.

"Stop!" I tell him. "I love you Rage. I love you and Kasey more than you know. The two of you have become my entire world. Well, until these two are born. I'm sorry that it took me a minute to respond, you just surprised me by saying it in front of people. Don't ever doubt my love for you and your daughter though."

Without giving him a chance to respond, I lean in and kiss him. I pour every ounce of love I feel for him into the kiss. There will never be room for doubt where my love for him and Kasey is concerned. Finally, he pulls away and I can see the smile on his face, the love shining from his eyes. Kasey is sitting next to us still and I pull her into our little circle. I place a kiss on her cheek and she tells me she loves me.

I'm just waking up and the smells permeating the room are absolutely amazing. My mouth is watering, and I can't wait to sample all the good food. I take care of my business and make my way out to join everyone else. The main room is flooded with all the men, old ladies, and kids. Grim made sure that other than Summer, the club girls are not here today. He is making sure that the ones that have no family are getting a Thanksgiving dinner though.

"You're up!" Kasey hollers, alerting everyone to the fact I just entered the main room.

I see the old ladies making their way to the kitchen and I follow them there after waving my hello to Kasey. Skylar is just pulling the turkey out of the oven and the rest of us are taking the rest of the food out to the tables. The only thing I didn't expect to see is Riley coming to help us out. I'm still mad at her, but I guess if there's any day that I'm going to start working on forgiving her, today would be that day. So, I offer a small smile and make my way out to the main room with a dish in each hand.

We really outdid ourselves with all the food. There's turkey, mashed potatoes, cranberry sauce, green bean casserole, rolls, and of course the amazing desserts. Skylar and Whitney each made three different pies and I want to be a greedy bitch and have a slice of each. However, there's too many other people that might have an issue with that.

Turning to make my way back into the kitchen, I almost slam head first into Riley. Thankfully, she's quicker on her feet than me and she manages to move out of the way before we can collide. I can see Rage watching the interaction between us from the corner of my eye. I know that he'd be over here in a heartbeat if he felt I was upset in any way by her presence. But, she's a guest here even if she is being kept away from phones and all other contact to the outside world. So far, I haven't heard about her making a single complaint about that. In fact, she seems to be almost thriving without the worry and stress on her shoulders. Turning, I smile at my man and continue to head back in the kitchen.

Just as we're bringing out the last of the dishes, and Joker has finished carving the turkey, everyone is taking their seats. A few of the men are rounding up the last of the kids with the help of Jameson and Anthony. Even though these two little boys aren't yet teenagers, I can already see that they are going to follow in the steps of their fathers and the rest of the men of the club. It's amazing to see the next generation of these men. Especially as the rest of the little boys get older. Jameson and Anthony are going to have them doing the same things that they do now.

"Penny for your thoughts?" Rage asks, coming up behind me and wrapping his arms around me.

"I was just thinking how amazing it is to see Jameson and Anthony protect the kids and make sure that as the boys get older that they're supposed to do the same thing. Our kids won't have any better role models than your brothers," I tell him, placing my hand over his.

"It is amazin' to watch them. Jameson has been doin' it for as long as I've been back here. Anthony followed in his footsteps as soon as Glock brought them back here."

We watch for a few minutes more before we take our seats at the table. Skylar stands up and says that this year we're going to go around the table and tell everyone what we're thankful for. I sit and listen as each person tells us what means the most to them. When it gets to my turn, I sit there and remain quiet for a minute.

"I'm thankful that I've finally been reunited with my family. I've missed you more than you'll ever know

Whitney and I'm glad that we're back together again. I'm glad to now have an extended family and the love of my life by my side. Rage and Kasey have become my entire universe and I can't thank you enough for loving me and giving us two new additions to our little family. Finally, I'm thankful that even though we started out based on a lie, I have Riley back in my life. We may not be as close as we were before, but I'm hoping with time we'll get there," I say, being pulled against Rage's side while he kisses my temple.

"I'm thankful that Keegan was brought into my life. She's my entire world and I can't wait to see our love grow even more as we spend the rest of our lives lovin' one another. I have Kasey back and don't have to worry about anythin' regardin' her. She's got a great role model with all the old ladies here, but especially my firefly. And, I'm glad that I found all of you and now have a bigger family than I could've ever dreamed possible."

Everyone continues to go around the table until we get to Riley. She looks directly at me and I can already see tears glistening in her eyes. I know that this is hitting her hard with me not really speaking to her. It was just a complete shock to learn that she was actually going to through with handing me over to my father and Sam. I'm glad that she didn't and I'm really trying to realize that she didn't have to change her mind and have my back. I'm sure we don't even know what truly happened to her as a result of her betrayal.

"I'm thankful that you all have taken me in. It doesn't matter to me that I can't go anywhere or talk on the phone. You've eliminated any threat against me and made sure that I am being honest when I say I love Keegan like a sister and I want to protect her and not harm her or let those animals get their hands on her. One day I hope that we'll be able to get some of what we used to have back."

Riley was the last person to go and I know that I have tears in my eyes. I'm not going to let them fall though. Her words hit home, and I know that eventually I'll be giving her another chance. It just won't be today. I can't risk anything with the twins I'm carrying and Kasey being around me. Not to mention the rest of the kids that are around here. I'd never forgive myself if anything happened to them because of me. I wouldn't be able to live with myself.

We all devour the food in front of us. The prospects are eating at a table closer to the kids in case they need help or want seconds. All the kids are laughing, having fun, and eating the food placed in front of them. You can see, and hear, the innocence of them. It's something that I'd give every day to hear from the kids around us. They may act big and tough, but they're still innocent in most things. The important things. I didn't get to have that as a child and it warms my heart to see all of the love and protection of the children belonging to the club.

"I don't know about the rest of you," Skylar starts. "I'm going to go lay down for a little bit before we go shopping. Darcy will be here soon, and I can't wait to see what happens this time!"

The men all groan at remembering some of the things that have happened with Darcy around. Especially involving Wood. I haven't seen them in person, but the girls have told me the stories. Now, I'm glad that Rage didn't beat his ass when I was in Benton Falls. It seems that he's on the verge of that from Crash and Trojan. Knowing that Darcy is coming here, I know that the two men will be accompanying her. Let the games begin, I think to myself. I can't wait to see these shenanigans first hand.

"I'm going to follow your lead," I tell her and Rage.

He follows me up to our room with Kasey hot on his heels. She's going to want to spend time with us before Pops and Alice take the kids for the night. They're all having a sleepover in the game room. Pops said that Alice already had a bunch of movies ready to bring along with popcorn and other drinks and snacks. I don't know where these kids are going to put this food in their tiny bellies, but I'm sure they'll find the room. They always seem to.

"Keegan, are you okay?" Kasey asks me, climbing up on the bed next to me.

"Yeah, why?" I ask, pulling her into my side.

"You sleep a lot now. Are the babies hurting you?"

"They're not hurting me baby. They just take a lot out of me. So, for a while, I'm going to be tired. But, I'll still have time to spend with you."

Kasey looks at me for a few minutes before settling down next to me. She snuggles into me and I love this time. Rage sits on the bed next to us and rubs his daughter's back. Once he realizes that she's asleep, when her chatter about anything and everything ceases, he brushes my hair away from my face and gazes down into my eyes.

"You sleep, and I'll wake you up when it's time to get ready," he tells me. "I'm gonna go make sure a few guys from Dander Falls get here. Darcy's drivin' them crazy."

"Okay babe," I tell him, laying my hand on his cheek. "I love you."

"Love you too," he tells me, giving me a kiss before heading out of the door.

I watch my man leave the room and get settled in. Kasey is curled up into my side fast asleep and as I move, she snuggles in deeper to me. Even in sleep she has a hand resting on my stomach. It's adorable the way that she always wants to be touching where the babies are resting. I've never really been around kids because of the situation I found myself in with Sam and my dad. Living with Kasey and experiencing life with her on a daily basis is the most amazing experience of my life. Rage in the mix is just the icing on the cake.

Waking up, I hear a ton of commotion coming from the common room. Something major must be happening to cause me to hear it all the way in the room. Looking down, I see Kasey is still passed out. I slowly get out from under her arm so I can quickly get her things ready to spend time with Alice and Pops.

Before I get too far, the door to Rage's room bursts open. Thinking that it's him, I look out the door to see what's going on. Instead of seeing him, I see the girls standing in the doorway. They're all laughing, giggling, and giving Darcy a hard time. Must be the commotion was because of her and the guys. I can't wait to see what happens when we go out shopping with them.

"Are you almost ready to go Keegan?" Darcy asks, laughing.

"Yeah. I just need to finish getting Kasey's things ready to go. Where are the guys?" I ask.

"They're trying to get the fucking cavemen under control. They think they're going to control what I do when we're out," Darcy answers.

I can't help the smirk on my face as I imagine what they were doing to make Darcy pissed off. Well, not so much because they always seem to do something to get under her skin. Now, I know that Darcy is going to go out of her way to make them get all worked up. This is going to be a fun night. Let the games begin!

Quickly I finish packing the bags, jump in the shower to get ready, and make my way out to common room after checking on Kasey. The rest of the girls are waiting for me drinking coffee, eating something, and hanging out in the kitchen. I grab a bowl of cereal and some toast so that I can put something in my stomach. Having more turkey and all that other food is going to make me want to take a nap again.

Sitting down next to Darcy, I listen to her telling everyone what's been going on with the guys. They apparently decided that she wasn't going to be trying on any clothes tonight, she can't be anywhere near Wood, and they're going to be on her like crazy to make sure she stays out of trouble. I know that I wouldn't be able to handle their overbearing sense when it comes to Darcy. She wants to have fun and be the life of the party when it comes to the girls. Crash and Trojan want her to be sedate and calm, not herself.

"So, are we bringing Riley with us?" Bailey asks.

All of a sudden, everyone looks to me. I'm not sure what they want me to say. If she wants to come, she can. If she chooses not to, she can sit here with the prospects or something. Riley isn't an enemy, she's just not as close to me as she was before. No matter what happens, she'll be in my heart because when no one else was there for me Riley was. Now, I need to make sure that she's being true and not secretly working for him.

"I don't know why everyone is looking at me to figure it out. It's her decision and she's the only one that can make it. Am I going to complain and bitch if she goes? No. I'm just going to be leery about spending time with her until I know for sure that she's not working with Sam and my dad," I tell the girls.

"Then I guess I'll go see what she wants to do," Bailey tells us, leaving the kitchen.

The rest of us finish what we're doing so that we can leave. Before too long I see Bailey enter the kitchen again followed by Riley. She looks amazing and ready to take on the world. But then, she always has. It's only because I know her so well that I see the pain she has hidden behind her eyes. I want to know what's happened to her to cause so much pain, but I'm not ready to do that yet. It's going to take a lot of time. And proof that she's being one hundred percent honest about not helping the men after me.

We managed to get out of the clubhouse without too much chaos ensuing. There was one point that I thought Darcy was about to castrate one of her Neanderthals, but she quickly escaped into Woods waiting vehicle and locked them out. I've never seen two grown men turn that particular shade of red, more a purple really, then when Crash and Trojan realized she wasn't going to give in to them. Rage and the rest of the guys were shaking their heads in frustration because we might not have been helping the situation at all. Then we were all laughing so hard that they had to practically lift us into the cars and trucks we were taking.

Somehow, Riley ended up riding with Rage, Gage, and I. I'm not going to bitch and whine about it. Maybe it's a sign that we're supposed to start moving on and getting back to where we were before. So, I'll give it a shot and see what happens tonight.

"Thanks for letting me ride with you guys," Riley tells us.

"It's not a problem," Rage responds, pulling out behind Joker and Cage. "Riley, this is Gage. Gage, meet firefly's friend Riley."

"It's nice to meet you," they both respond.

Looking in my mirror, I can see the sidelong glances that Riley keeps giving Gage. This is interesting because I've never seen her be shy around a single soul in her life. Even when she's had someone beating the shit out of her, she'd protect me and keep it going on her so I wouldn't be touched. In many ways, Riley always had my back. I need to let go of this and let us both move on. I need to be there for her to help her heal the pain she's feeling and hiding behind her eyes.

Riley used to be so vibrant and full of life. Now, she's almost a shell of her former self from what I've seen. There's a pain and darkness hidden behind her eyes that was never there before. Something happened to this girl after I left, and I hope that she still trusts in me enough to get it out. No matter what happens between us, I will always have her back. Riley has had my back on more than one occasion and I'll never be able to pay her back for it. If I'm the only one that she has to lean on, then I'll be that for her.

"Riley, I'm going to try to move past what I've found out since you showed up. It still might not happen immediately, but I see the changes in you and I want to be there to help you," I tell her.

"I know it's going to take time Keegan. And one day I'll let you know what's going on. Just not today. Tonight, is about shopping and having fun."

I turn back around in my seat and settle in for the trip. The guys are still taking precautions since no more letters or flowers have arrived. We honestly have no clue what their next move is going to be. Rage didn't want to let me come tonight, but there was no way I was missing out on this shit. Not after what I've heard happens when Darcy is out with everyone.

Rage

So far, we've been to about three stores. Crash and Trojan are moping around because Darcy has put them in their place multiple times, in front of everyone. Now apparently, we're going into some lingerie store and I'm not looking forward to seeing what is going to happen in here. Especially when I see all of the stuff that I'd love to see firefly wearing.

Before any of us can blink, the women are going through the store like mini tornadoes. They're going from rack to rack finding what they think are the cutest little outfits to tease their men in. As soon as they're done choosing the items they want to try on, I hear a few of the old ladies commenting that there aren't enough dressing rooms with all the other customers in the store. So, they decide to double up and go in the rooms together. Catching Keegan's eye, I see a wide smile break out across her face. Darcy is standing next to her and I see them heading towards the same dressing room. Fuck my life!

I'm moving closer to the dressing rooms as I see Wood pacing back and forth in front of the doors. He's making sure that no one can get to our women. I appreciate the gesture, but I want my eyes on Keegan. If she needs me, I want to be right there to help her. It's my woman, my babies, and my job to protect and love her. Wood is a brother from another club, and I trust him with my life. Keegan is another story though.

Before I can get to the dressing rooms, I see their door open. Wood turns around and everything seems to happen in slow motion. The girls try to come through the door at the same time, only my girl gets tripped up somehow. Wood makes a move to catch her at the same time Darcy does. I'm not quite sure what happened after that but before anyone can make a move, the three are sprawled out on the floor. Wood is on the bottom of the pile, Darcy is on top of him face to face with him, and Keegan ended up on her back on top of Darcy.

I immediately rush over to them and check my girl over. She's laughing so hard that I see tears running down her cheeks. Helping her up, I'm still checking her over and she is my entire focus. I don't notice when Crash and Trojan make their way over to us. Well, until they start yelling at Darcy to get her ass off of Wood.

"Are you fuckin' kiddin' me?" Crash bellows. "Every fuckin' time you two are around one another, you end up all over each other."

"Go the fuck away Neanderthal!" Darcy yells, pulling herself off Wood.

"Firecracker, you know you're goin' to be ours. Why keep fightin' it?" Trojan asks.

"I never said I was going to be yours," she says before Wood grunts. "Oh! I'm so sorry!"

Looking over, I see Wood holding his dick. I guess in her rush to get off him, she put her hand there and pushed herself up. I'm cringing at the pain he must be in right now. Crash and Trojan start laughing their asses off because I'm sure they think that's what he deserves after having his hands on their woman. Again.

"Firefly, are you sure you're okay?" I ask, seeing that she's calmed down a little bit.

"I'm perfect. The babies are fine. Wood made sure to turn me somehow so I landed on my back. It's not like I landed on the floor." Keegan starts laughing again.

"This is even better than what everyone has told me about these three."

I can't help but laugh. Keegan is having a good time and she's getting to witness the hot mess that is Crash, Trojan, Darcy, and Wood. She's been waiting to see this shit first-hand. I love that she looks like a kid in a candy store right now. This is how my girl should look every day of her life. If I have my way, she will.

"Alright, are you gettin' this hot as fuck outfit?" I ask, taking in the corset she's wearing with thigh highs and matching G-string.

"I'm thinking about it. It's just going to sit in a drawer somewhere until I have the babies, but I love it."

I tell her to get the outfit and whatever else she took in the room with her. She can give me a private showing later on at the clubhouse. While she goes in to get dressed, I go and grab a few more of the corsets. If she likes them, I'm going to get them for her.

We've been shopping for hours and I'm ready to go back to the clubhouse. I know Keegan is too. She's starting to move slower and leaning on me more and more. Looking over at Grim, I motion to my girl and that's all I need to do. He knows that it's time to go and starts rounding everyone up. Noticing that we're passing by a jeweler, I pass Keegan off to Bailey and the rest of the girls to go get her something to eat and drink for the ride home.

Walking in the store, an overly made-up woman approaches me. I'm not paying any attention to her though. My only goal is picking out the perfect ring for firefly. This woman just doesn't get the hint though. Out of the corner of my eye, I see a man and make my way over to him. Getting closer, I see that it's Craig. He's a guy I met when I was younger, and we talk for a few minutes before he asks me what I'm looking for.

Within a few minutes, Craig has shown me the perfect ring. It's not too big and it fit's Keegan's personality completely. The ring is platinum with sapphires and diamonds surrounding the band. In the center is a diamond that's held up by little skulls. I've never seen a ring with skulls on it, but I know my girl loves skulls. She's already shown me a few things that she wants to put in the house when it's done.

"Where did you disappear to baby?" she asks me when I find them in the food court.

"I saw someone I know from way back. We talked for a few minutes. I would've taken you with me, but our babies needed to eat."

"Oh. Next time then."

And just like that my girl proves why I fall more and more in love with her every single day. I think the only thing I could do to hurt or piss her off is cheating on her or treating her like shit. Neither thing would ever happen, but she's just so relaxed and goes with the flow.

"Did all the bags make it to the truck?" she asks, finishing her pretzel.

"Yeah. The guys have been makin' regular trips out with them all. I don't know how Gage and Riley are goin' to fit in the backseat with everythin' we bought."

"They can ride on the roof if they have to," she says. "Everything was for you, Kasey, and the babies."

"I'm not complainin' at all firefly."

Pretty soon we're all loading up in the vehicles and making our way back to the clubhouse. Pops and Alice never once contacted us, so I hope everything is okay with them and the kids. Pops can handle them, but I'm still getting to know Alice. To me, she's still and unknown and I'm worried about my daughter with everything going on.

"I want to take a nap when we get back," Keegan announces to the rest of us. "I'm beat and sore."

"If you were gettin' sore, why didn't you tell me baby?" I ask.

"Because it's nothing I can't handle."

"I know that. But, it's not somethin' you have to deal with either."

The rest of the ride is silent. Well, except for the muted conversation coming from the backseat between Riley and Gage. If you ask me, I think Riley will end up moving to Dander Falls. Gage and her seem to be hitting it off. He needs some good in his life. Riley just might be the person to give that to him.

Chapter Six

Keegan

TIME IS FLYING BY AND IT'S JUST a few days before Christmas. The house is almost finished, and Rage really wanted us to be moved in before Christmas day. I don't see that happening, but who knows. He just wanted Kasey to be in our home, so she could open everything there and give us a little bit of time to be a family before meeting with everyone else in the club. Personally, I don't care where we are as long as we're together.

I'm almost four months along and my stomach is getting bigger every day. Kasey now gives the babies kisses and lovin' every day. She says that her babies are going to know their big sister. This little girl weaves her way into my heart a little more each and every day. Especially when she sees me getting tired and gives me an excuse to lay down. Kasey now tells me that it's her nap time and she wants to lay down with me. We both fall asleep and she makes sure that her little hands are on my belly, so she can hold the babies while we all nap.

Rage has been acting weird and I'm not sure what's going on. As far as I know there haven't been any more notes or flowers delivered. He wouldn't tell me these days if there had been though. His main concern is keeping me relaxed and stress free as much as possible. I love him for it, but it's really bothering me that he won't talk to me about whatever is bothering him. I've tried talking to him about it and he just tells me everything is fine. I know it's not based on his actions and the look I see in his eyes sometimes.

Honestly, I'm beginning to get worried that he's changed his mind and doesn't want me around anymore. I'm tired of the uncertainty so I'm going to get to the bottom of this right now. Hefting my ass out of bed, I check on Kasey to make sure she's still sleeping and go in search of my man. After looking all over, I finally find him in the main room. The sight before me takes my breath away.

In the middle of the main room is a chair, in front of the empty chair stands Rage. He's dressed like he's ready to go out and he's nervous. I can tell by the shifting back and forth from foot to foot. His head is facing the floor when I enter and everyone in the room doesn't make a sound as I make my way over to him. I place my hand on his cheek and he raises his head to look me in the eyes. After a minute, he helps me sit in the chair and drops to one knee in front of me. Tears are already falling from my eyes as he kisses me softly and takes my hand.

"I know you've been tryin' to figure out what's goin' on with me and all sorts of crazy ass thoughts have been goin' through your head. I'm sorry for that firefly. I love you more than I'll ever be able to tell you. Kasey, you, and our babies are the most important people in the world to me. Without you by my side, I can't do what has to be done. Firefly, you've become the air I breathe and the light to my dark. You calm me down with just a look and I know you were sent here for me. For our daughter and me. Would you do me the honor of bein' my old lady and makin' it legal in the eyes of the outside world?" Rage asks, holding his breath as he waits for my answer.

"Yes," comes out a whisper with all the emotion I'm feeling right now.

"Yes?" he asks.

I nod my head as he slides the ring on my finger. Everyone around us starts hollering and moving closer to offer their congratulations. I can see that Rage wants to get me alone, so I make my way closer to him and grab his hand. As I go to lead him up to our room in the clubhouse, he changes direction and moves us towards the back door. I let him lead me where he wants to go.

As soon as we make the short walk to our house, Rage picks me up and carries me through the door. He doesn't give me a chance to look at anything as we move towards the back of the house. Opening the door to the master bedroom, he carries me over to a bed and places me in the middle. For a minute he does nothing but look down at me.

"You've made me the happiest man in the world," he tells me.

Rage begins kissing me and placing kisses all over my exposed skin. While he's doing this, I feel him beginning to strip me. In a matter of minutes, I'm naked and reaching up to undress my man, the love of my life. Once he's naked, he climbs into bed with me. I see him holding himself above me, not putting any pressure on my stomach.

We're gazing in one another's eyes as he slowly enters me. I arch up to meet him and pull him down, so I can kiss him. There is no rushing or trying to find our release quick this time. Rage is showing me how much he loves me as he slowly slides in and out of me. I wrap my legs around him and don't try to go any faster than what he wants. I've never been with him like this, and it's nice.

"I love you firefly."

"I love you!" I tell him, feeling my release begin to build.

Sensing that I'm getting close, Rage leans his head down and takes one nipple in his mouth. Sucking and biting to get me there even faster. I arch up into his mouth and bring my entire body closer to his. Without warning, my release breaks, and crashes over me. I yell out his name and feel him follow close behind me.

As we're both coming down, he places gentle kisses along my neck and pulls out of me. Instantly I feel the loss and curl myself around him. We lay there until we can both breathe normally again. Rage then leads me into the master bathroom where I stand in complete awe. This bathroom is a dream come true. There's a huge tub we can both fit in, a shower that another six people can fit in, his and her sinks below a full mirror and medicine cabinet, and shelves for towels and whatever else I want to put in here. I've already been told the decorating is completely up to me.

On the back of the door is a robe. Rage goes over and moves it out of the way showing me that my rag is hanging below it. My mouth drops open and the tears once again start forming in my eyes.

"This is amazing!" I gush out as Rage starts filling the tub.

"You deserve it firefly. We deserve it. We're goin' to take a bath so I can clean you up and then go share the news with our daughter."

"Sounds good babe."

Needless to say, Kasey was thrilled with our news. She hugged and kissed us both, not letting go for a long time. There were tears in her eyes when she finally let go of us. I sat on the bed and her dad knelt down beside her.

"What's the matter baby girl?" I ask her, brushing her hair out of her face.

"I'm gonna haves a mama that loves me now," is her simple reply. This little girl kills me and brings me back to life at the same time.

"I will always love you Kasey," I tell her.

"And we'll all love the babies when they get here," she says, sitting on her dad's knee.

"We will," he answers. "Keegan and I have enough love for everyone in our little family. No matter how many kids we have. You'll always be our baby girl since you were the first one born though."

Kasey wraps her arms around his neck and buries her face in his neck. I can tell she's crying and that she loves that we're going to be a family. Her world revolves around her dad and her extended family of the club. Now, it includes me, and I'm honored that I'm included in her little circle.

It's the day before Christmas and the old ladies and I have been finishing up wrapping our gifts. I'm not quite sure how it happens, but we get on the topic of adult stores. Most of us have been to them at one point or another in our life. Whitney and myself have not though. There was never any time for me when I was too busy hiding from Sam and my dad.

"You two are shitting me!" Bailey calls out. "We need to go. Now!"

The rest of the women nod their heads 'yes'. Bailey starts picking everything up and the rest of us follow suit. I wasn't planning on going today, but apparently, we are. I'm not sure how this is going to turn out, but I'll go with the flow and see what happens.

"We need one more person," Maddie states, pulling out her phone. "Darcy, it's Maddie. We're making a trip to an adult store, you in?"

None of us can hear her response, but I'm sure she's all in. Darcy seems like the type of person that is down for anything. And we all know that when she's around, we're all bound to have fun.

"I don't want anyone to tell the guys where we're going," Bailey says. "We're just telling them that we're going to the store. I know that Rage for sure is going to go. Wood will probably go. If Darcy comes, Crash and Trojan will be up her ass. Maybe a prospect will come too. Mums the word until we pull in. They're just going to have to ride bitch and see where we go."

We all go our separate ways to get ready. Rage is asking me where we're going, and I just tell him that we need some last-minute things so we're heading to the store. As anticipated, he throws his coat on and waits for me to finish. I hold out my hand and Rage just looks at me.

"I want to drive. Please baby?" I ask, pulling out the pouty lip and puppy dog eyes.

After taking a minute to think it over, he hands over the keys. We head back to the main room and see everyone else waiting for us. Wood, Grim, and a prospect are sitting by the door so I'm guessing they're making the trip with us. Bailey is separating everyone up, so we only have to take two vehicles. I hold up the keys to let her know that I'm driving Rage's SUV.

Before too long we head out and I follow Bailey. Grim sure wasn't happy about her driving, but he's letting her have her way. I'm sure there will be some form of payment from her because of this. Laughing to myself, I'm thinking I'll end up in the same predicament later on. I'm all for it!

The store we're going to is halfway between Clifton Falls and Dander Falls. Once we finally pull in, Darcy is getting out of her car with Crash and Trojan. She doesn't look happy at all. Especially when I see her storming over to us.

"This better be fun since I've got dip shit one and two with me."

"You've never been to one either?" Bailey asks, looking over at Grim to see his reaction.

"Nope."

"Bailey, you seriously had us all come out so you could go shoppin' for new toys?" Grim asks, walking closer to us.

"Yep. There are a few here that have never been to an adult store. We needed to rectify that immediately. Besides, you know you're going to like it when we get back home."

There's nothing Grim can say to that so he shuts his mouth and motions for us to lead the way. As soon as we're all through the door, I stop and stare at everything before me. On one side there are movies, a lot of movies. In the middle of the store are racks and racks of every type of lingerie you could want. There's even stripper heels and I head for them. Out of the corner of my eye, I see half the girls go to the other side of the store where toys and things like that are. I'll get there eventually, but I want to look at these shoes first.

One pair grabs my attention immediately. They're clear and upon closer inspection, there's a switch on the inside between the back of the shoe and the heel. Reading the paper in front of them, I see that they light up. My eyes about pop out of my head because I know I want these shoes now. I don't care that they're stripper shoes, I just may have an addiction to buying shoes. Even if I never wear them.

"You like these, firefly?" Rage asks, coming up behind me.

"I do. I want them so bad Rage."

"Then find your size and get them."

"I'll probably never wear them." I say, trying to talk myself out of buying these shoes.

"You'll wear them. Remember, you still owe me a private viewin' party of what you bought before. And, I'm sure there's goin' to be more bought tonight."

I look at my man and I can already see the lust and determination in his eyes. Looking below the shoes, I find my size and hesitantly pull the box off the shelf. Rage takes them from me before I can change my mind. He then leads me to the racks of clothing. There are a few cute baby doll nighties that I pick out and add to his arms. Finally, I take a deep breath and make my way over to the section the rest of the girls are in.

"You're one of the ones aren't you firefly?" Rage asks, coming up directly behind me.

"Yeah. I don't even know where to begin looking."

"Wherever you want to. Lead the way baby."

Making my way over to Darcy, I see her looking at vibrators of all different shapes and sizes. I can already feel my face turning red from embarrassment. Darcy's face is so red it's almost purple. I'm just not sure if it has to do with everything we're looking at, or that Crash and Trojan are standing directly behind her. There's only one other person in the store and he's making sure to stay away from us.

Darcy has a small blue vibrator in her hand and she's looking it over. Once she sees me, I can see her relax a little bit. My face must give it away that I've also never been in this kind of store. She hands it over to me and I start looking at it. Rage whispers that since he's bigger than that it would basically be a waste of time to get that one. I blush worse and hand it back to my friend.

Without saying a word, Darcy and I make our way through the store together. If we look puzzled about anything, the guys are helpful enough to explain what we're looking at. Who knew there was all this shit? A few times, I thought Darcy was going to pass out when one of her men got real close and started going into detail what they would do to her with one item or another. She's got it so bad for these two it's not funny.

We're finally almost relaxed when we get to the rack that has all sorts of party favors and things like that on it. Darcy immediately picks up a bag of candy that's shaped like a dick. They're different colors and I can see her wanting to burst out laughing. I know I'm getting some so I pick a bag up and hand it to Rage. He doesn't even bat an eye as he adds it to the growing pile.

The girls are trying to hide something as Darcy and I get closer to them. I'm not sure what's going on, and I really don't know that I want to know. Bailey and Grim walk away before we can find out what's going on, but I'm sure we'll find out before too long. Skylar leads us over to this other rack and there's a ton of paddles, whips, and things like that on there. One paddle in particular catches my eye. It's black and is covered in little skulls. I really want this. Picking it up, I hand it to Rage and he just looks at me.

I'm not really sure what I'm getting myself into with this, but we'll find out soon. Especially with the look on Rage's face as he's looking at the latest item I've added to the pile. He starts looking at the other ones like it and chooses one that has hearts on it too. Must be one for when I'm naughty and one when I'm good. Darcy glances over and sees the growing pile in his arms and I swear her face turns another whole level of red. Hey, I'm down to try anything once and this is a fun shopping trip for me. I'm learning all sorts of new things tonight.

"So, you think we need to get firecracker one or two of those?" Trojan asks Crash.

"Like hell you will!" she cries out, louder than intended I'm sure.

"Yeah, I think we need a few of them. That way we can have one handy most everywhere we are," Crash states.

Darcy shuts her mouth at that and storms back over towards the racks of different colored vibrators. Just as she goes to round the corner, Wood comes from the opposite side and they run right into one another. Both go crashing to the floor and the display follows them down. I stand there in shock for a minute before and uncontrollable fit of laughter bursts from me. Even the menacing glances from Crash and Trojan don't stop the laughter from flowing. Not from a single one of us.

"Are you serious?" Trojan yells out. "Every. Single. Time."

Darcy is sputtering and trying to get up and away from Wood and the toys laying on the floor. I think it's because one or two of the display models may have turned on and are vibrating their way across the floor. Wood is still laying on the floor looking up at the ceiling looking like he wishes it would open up and pull him away from yet another incident.

Crash and Trojan stalk their way over to the two and I can see that this isn't going to end well. Wood is about to get his ass kicked and no one is doing anything to stop it. I look up at Rage and plead with him to step in. He just gives me a slight shake of his head to let me know he's not getting involved in this mess. So, I make my way over to the foursome to see what kind of damage control I can do.

"Darcy, are you okay?" I ask, trying to snap her two Neanderthals out of their stupor.

"I think I am," she says, looking at the mess all over the floor.

We both bend down and begin to pick the display up. The men see what we're doing, and they put a stop to it. Instead, Crash, Trojan, and Wood all work together to pick the vibrating toys up and put them back on the rack. Once again, I can't help giggling at the sight of these alpha males picking up a bunch of toys while the two of us look on in amusement. Before too long, Darcy is joining in on the laughter followed closely by the guys. In one quick decision, I managed to break the tension and stop Wood from having to drink out of a straw for the foreseeable future.

"Thank you, firefly," Wood whispers to me as they put the last of the toys up.

Bailey walks over to us and lets us know that we need to get back to the clubhouse so we all make our way towards the register to cash out. Wood makes sure to stay far away from Darcy for the remainder of our time in the store. I really can't blame him for that. Darcy is still sticking close to me and that's fine. I don't think she wants to see what the two men behind me are purchasing. Let's just say that she's going to have some eye-opening experiences when she finally gives in to the men.

As soon as we're all checked out, I walk Darcy to her car. The men are following closely behind us. I hug her close to me and whisper that I'm always there for her. She tells me that one of these days we need to get together and go out. Even if it's just the two of us. I know we haven't known one another long, but she is quickly coming one of my good friends. Darcy is someone that pulls you in with how outrageous she is. Then you just have no choice but to fall in love with her. Probably what happened to the two men following her around like little lost puppy dogs.

Rage leads me back to the SUV and loads me in. Soon we're on our way back to the clubhouse so we can get Kasey ready for bed and finish whatever is left. Eventually Rage will put everything under the tree in the house he got somehow. Tonight is the first night we'll be in our new home. It's not decorated yet. But, we have some furniture there and Kasey's room is already completed. I can't wait to get the inside done and have everything where it needs to go.

Rage

Climbing out of the warmth of our bed and being wrapped around Keegan, I make my way to where we stored the presents. It won't be too long before Kasey is waking us up and I need to get everything under the tree. Keegan is still trying to figure out how I managed to get a tree, put it up, and get it decorated before she even stepped foot in the house. Having prospects around is a wonderful thing. I told them what I wanted, and they made sure to get it done.

Even though I told my girl I didn't want, or need, anything for Christmas, she made sure to get me stuff. Honestly, I have everything I could possibly want between my daughter, the love of my life, and two new babies on the way. The only thing that can't go under the tree is one of the gifts I got for Keegan. Without her knowledge, I finished the nursery and I'm going to show it to her as soon as all the gifts under the tree are opened.

I take a few bites of the cookies that Skylar made and drink some of the milk that Kasey wanted to leave out for Santa. She was adamant that we do this and I'm not going to break her heart by not doing it. I cherish the days that prove how innocent my baby girl truly is. This isn't going to last much longer, but I'm going to take what I can get for as long as I can.

As soon as I'm done, I make my way back into Keegan. She's still asleep and I watch her for a few minutes. My girl is so relaxed and peaceful right now. There's no worry about what the two assholes looking for her are going to do or where they are. Right now, I would do anything to keep this look on her face as long as I can. Realistically, I know that's not going to happen. One day soon these two men are going to make their move and I hope that she's by my side when they do.

"Daddy! Keegan! Santa's here! Santa's here!" Kasey comes barreling in our room, jumping on my side of the bed in her excitement.

"He is?" Keegan asks, wiping the sleep from her eyes and yawning.

"Yes! Come sees!" she says, jumping off the bed and running for the door.

"We'll be right there," I tell her, pulling the covers back and reaching for my sweats.

I watch Keegan head for the bathroom and finish getting dressed while she's doing her thing. Once she's back in the room, she throws one of my tees on over her shorts and we head out to find Kasey sitting in front of the tree waiting for us. She's not waiting patiently as she's bouncing on her little legs, eyeing all the gifts under the tree. I know she's trying to decide what to open first.

"Why don't I hand out the presents and you sit by Keegan?" I ask her.

"Okay daddy," she says, climbing on the couch next to firefly.

I pick out a gift for each of us and our day begins. It shouldn't take us that long to open everything. Then, I can show them both the nursery. Kasey saw part of it one day and has been pissed at me ever since. I wouldn't let her back in the door to spoil the surprise for Keegan. Today, she can finally stop being mad and fall in love with it.

"Okay ladies," I begin once the last gift has been opened. "There's one more gift. It's too big to fit under the tree so you'll have to follow me."

"Where is it daddy?" Kasey asks, trying to figure out what I'm talking about.

"It's in the house still. Let's go."

Leading them down the hallway, I stop in front of the door Keegan and I decided would be the best for a nursery. Opening it up, I let the two ladies in my life enter before I walk in behind them. Keegan gasps and I can see the tears as she turns to look at me. Kasey is wandering around, touching everything in sight.

The walls of the nursery are painted a soft yellow since we'll have a boy and girl in here. On one wall, there is space left for the cribs to sit one end to the other. One crib is going to be decorated in pinks and teddy bears with the ultrasound picture saying 'I'm a Girl' above it. The other crib will be decorated in blues and motorcycles with the picture saying 'I'm a Boy' hanging above it. There's a changing table, a few diapers and outfit's hanging in the closet already. Little things that I've picked up along the way. Sitting by the windows are two glider rockers. This way we can both sit in here and take care of our children together.

"This is amazing!" Keegan tells me, wrapping her arms around me and laying a kiss on me. "It's even better than anything I could have picked out myself. Thank you so much!"

"You don't have to thank me, firefly. This is for our children and I wanted it to be special. It's the best that I could do, and I'm glad that you like it."

"I don't like it. I love it!" she tells me, finally walking around.

I stand back and watch her take in every detail. The love and astonishment shining from her eyes tells me that I've managed to make her day. This isn't something that either one of my girls was expecting to see today and I'm glad that I could make this special for them. Especially Keegan. Without her saying a word, you can tell she's someone that hasn't had a whole lot of good in her life. I'm glad that she chose me to bring that good to her.

We've had our time as a family to celebrate the holidays. Now, it's time to head over to the clubhouse and celebrate with the rest of our family. The kids will get to open more gifts and then we'll have dinner. I'm sure at one point or another the party will turn wild. That's when I'll bring my girls back home and relax with them. We'll probably end up crashing in the living room and watching movies with bellies full of everything that Skylar and the rest of the women have spent days cooking.

On our walk over, we meet up with Whitney and Irish. Our two families enter the clubhouse together and it's already semi-controlled chaos. Kids are all over the place waiting for the last ones to get there so gifts can be opened. They're talking about what Santa has brought them and what they want to do with the rest of their day. Jamison and Anthony are kind of sitting back watching everyone. The same thing they always do.

"Daddy, can I plays with Zoey?" Kasey asks as soon as we get in the common room.

"Yeah."

She takes off running in the direction of Tank and Maddie's little girl. Anthony's eyes snap in the direction of my daughter and I'm wondering how much I'm going to have to pay attention to the two of them as they get older. Every one of us already know that Jamison and Zoey follow one another around. Wherever that little girl goes, he's not far behind her. I can easily see Anthony doing the same thing with my daughter. Looking across the room, I see that Glock has also witnessed the interaction between the two of them. He gives me a slight nod of his head to let me know that we'll all be watching them as they grow and start noticing the differences between the two of them.

"Keegan and Whitney, can you help us in the kitchen please?" Maddie calls out. She looks crazed and like something's on fire.

"Be right there," my girl responds.

Before Keegan leaves my side, she gives me a kiss that leaves me wanting more. There's no time for that now, but if she wants to play that game, we can definitely play that game. By the time I'm done with her, she'll be begging me to take her to our room here and have my way with her. And, I just so happen to have one of the paddles we bought last night here. Keegan really doesn't know what's she's getting into today.

Today has been long and the kids are starting to show that they're getting tired. I've been ready to leave for a while now, but Keegan has been having such a good time with her cousin and the rest of the old ladies that I couldn't bring myself to tell her I wanted to go home. Now, it's a different story. Kasey is more than ready to go home and it's showing. She's rubbing her eyes and not as active. I want to get her out of here before she starts to get grumpy. A grumpy Kasey is not a fun one. At all.

"You ready to go firefly?" I ask her, walking up behind the chair she's sitting in.

"Yeah," she responds, yawning and trying to hide it.

Irish, Whitney, and I laugh at her attempt. She didn't hide it at all and now I know for sure it's time to go. At this rate, she'll be asleep before I get our daughter into bed. Keegan needs to rest though so I'm not going to complain.

"Rage!" Grim calls out. "Need a minute."

Walking over to my president, I wonder what could possibly be going on now. I don't have to wait long as he leads me into his office and firmly shuts the door behind us. Cage and Joker are already in here and I know what I'm about to hear isn't going to be good.

"I want you, Keegan, and Kasey to stay here tonight. There's been someone in town askin' for Keegan. We can't be sure who it is right now, but I think it would be better for you to stay in the clubhouse tonight. Or until we find more information out." Grim tells me, and I understand where he's coming from. "At this point, your house is behind the fence, but we can keep more eyes on your family in here."

"I know. It's goin' to kill her since we've only stayed one night. But, I'm goin' to have to tell her what's goin' on. That's the only way I'm goin' to be able to convince her to stay here. That okay?"

"Yeah. We just wanted to let you know alone so you could figure out what you wanted to do." he responds.

"I'll take them to our room now then. She needs to sleep."

"Give you a half hour and then I want to call church."

I nod my head and make my way back over to Keegan. She can already tell something is going on from the look on my face. So, she stands up and makes her way over to Kasey. I lead them both back to our rooms in the clubhouse and we put our little girl to bed. As soon as we're in our room, I sit her down and tell her what Grim just let me know.

"So, they're starting to make their move?" she asks.

"It would appear so."

"What happens now?"

"I'm headin' to church where we'll discuss our next steps. I want you to get some sleep and I'll be back as soon as I can."

"Who's going to be here with us?"

"There's goin' to be a prospect outside the door. No one other than me will get in this room. I want you to lock the door and don't open it up for anyone."

"Okay."

Keegan lays down on the bed and I know before I get back, she'll be in pajamas. She's just going to take a few minutes to rest before taking a shower and getting ready for bed. Without her saying a word, I hand her one of my shirts, giver her a kiss, and make my way towards the door. Turning, I take one last look at her laying in our bed. Firefly turns her head towards me and gives me the smile she saves just for me. Before I decide to join her in bed, I open the door and leave the room. I lock it behind me and warn the prospect he'll suffer at least bodily harm if anything happens to my girls.

Chapter Seven

Rage

IT'S BEEN A FEW MONTHS SINCE Christmas and we still haven't heard a word from Keegan's dad and Sam. She's not allowed to go out alone and I'm spending most of my time with her. It's not that I don't trust my brothers to protect her and Kasey with their lives, it's that I want to be the one to be there. However, the main place she goes is to the doctor and that's it.

"Rage, I need to get out of this clubhouse today," Keegan announces as she enters our room from the bathroom. "I can't stand being cooped up anymore. Please, take me to get something to eat or something."

"I don't know firefly. I don't think it's a good idea."

"Is there anything I can do? It's starting to feel like the walls are closing in on me," she tells me, sitting on the bed.

"Let me talk to Grim and we'll see what he has to say. I'll be right back."

I find Grim in his office and I know that he's in a good mood today. He's got music blaring, his feet are kicked up, and he just looks relaxed. Quickly, I explain the situation to him and he thinks about it for a few minutes before answering me. I hate when he does this, but I know he's thinking about every possible scenario in advance of making any kind of decision.

"I guess you can. But, you're goin' to take Wood, Boy Scout, Cage, and Joker with you. Two in front, two in back. That understood?"

"Yes. Thank you."

Making my way back to our room, I quickly let the four men know that we're going to be leaving. They get ready as I'm going to get Keegan. I know Kasey's going to be mad that she can't go, but there's nothing I can do about that. Bailey and Skylar will keep her occupied for the short amount of time that we're gone though.

"Let's go firefly," I say entering the room.

"We can leave?" she asks, excitedly.

"Yeah. We have to get takeout and take four men with us, but we can go out. There and back. No extra stops and no sitting down to eat."

"I can handle that. Just need to get away for a few minutes."

We're all making our way out the door when a black van blows through the front gate and comes to a screeching halt in front of us. The sliding door on the side slams open and I know that these men are here for my girl. I push her back into Cage and Wood's waiting arms while the men inside reach out for her. Instead, they grab me and pull me into the van. Boy Scout and Joker are trying to pull me back out, but they aren't successful. The door slams shut as I'm thrown to my back. A black bag is thrown over my head and I can hear the anguished screams of Keegan as we speed away.

After my hands and feet are finally tied together, a hand snakes up under the bag and I can feel myself slipping away. The last thoughts I have are of my daughter and Keegan. Of the babies that I'm more than likely not going to ever see and have a hand in raising.

Keegan

"No!" I scream as I feel my body start to hit the ground.

Before I can make it all the way to the ground, Wood scoops me up and turns to head inside with me. we're heading in as the rest of the men are running outside to find out what's going on. I can hear myself still screaming and trying to wrench out of Wood's arms, but he's not letting go. I want nothing more than to go after the men that took the love of my life. That took Kasey's dad away from her.

"You need to calm down firefly. Please don't make me call the doc in to sedate you," Wood pleads with me.

There's no way I can calm down though. Rage just literally pushed me into the arms of these men so that they would take him in my place. Why the fuck would he do that? They're not after him, they're after me. He has no clue what they're going to do to him because he's not who Sam and my dad want. Eventually they're going to get to me anyway. Rage should've just let them take me.

"Wood, I need to get to him. Please let me go after him!" I scream out.

I can hear a door being pushed open, but I have no clue who's room we're at. Wood lays me down on the bed and the only thing I can think of is that I need to be with Kasey, but going after Rage at the same time. Before I can make any moves, I'm surrounded by more men and the old ladies. They're all trying to keep me in bed and warn me to calm down because of the babies. Unfortunately, I don't have any clue what I'm doing right now. I'm so scared and out of my mind with worry that I can't focus or concentrate on anything.

"Please, Keegan, you need to calm down!" Whitney says, trying to soothe me. "Please calm down. There's already guys going after Rage. We'll get him back."

"I-I-I need to b-b-be out there with them!" I gasp out between gasps and sobs.

"No!" Bailey says. "You need to be in here waiting for the men to do their jobs and being there for Kasey."

Without any further time, Kasey comes running in the door. Instantly she knows something is wrong. Climbing up in the bed with me, she wraps her little arms around my neck and buries her face. I know that she's going to be asking where her dad is and I'm not looking forward to having to answer that question. Honestly, I know when she finds out what happened, she's going to hate me. I basically took her dad away from her and her brother and sister. Who wouldn't hate me right now?

"Why's everyone look so sad?" she asks, looking around at all the adults in the room.

"Well, somethin's happened and your dad has to go away for a little while," Grim tells her. "He'll be back as soon as he can."

Kasey takes a minute to process what she was just told. She's not a stupid little girl and knows that's not the truth though. Anyone looking at all the adults in the room can see that it's not the truth. Instead of saying anything more on the subject, Kasey gets up and runs out of the room. She's been lied to and now she doesn't want to be around any of us.

"I got her," we hear from the doorway.

I look over through my tears and see Anthony standing there. He's looking at all of us and disappears without saying another word. I'm glad that he's going to be there for her right now. Even though I really want to, there's no way I can get past what just happened and be there for her when she's hurting and doesn't know what truly happened.

So, I turn over and put my back to everyone. I let the tears fall as I curl up in a fetal position. Hopefully everyone gets the hint and leaves me alone. I know I'm not going to get that lucky, but a girl can hope. Before letting myself fall asleep so I can forget the nightmare I'm living in, I turn on *Picture On The Dashboard* by Brantley Gilbert.

Chapter Eight

Rage

I CAN'T EVEN BEGIN TO TELL YOU how many days I've been in this fucked up situation. I'm hanging from a rafter in the ceiling of a warehouse and across the room is Riley. At first, I thought she had been lying to us and really was working with them. But, men came in and raped and tortured her right in front of me. There's no way she's working with them.

I've learned a lot about her in the moments that I'm conscious. She has a child that was ripped away from her. There's been no mention of the child's father, but I know that Sam has her baby. They've taunted her with that knowledge and what kind of future awaits her daughter. From the very beginning, Sam and Keegan's dad have tortured this poor girl. It wouldn't surprise me at all if one of them were the father of her daughter.

Riley is barely alive from the little that I can see of her. Hell, I'm not doing much better at this point. I've been beat several times, the threat of killing Kasey has been thrown in my face, and they've told me that they're going to go after every chapter of the Wild Kings. These slimy bastards can try all they want, I will be found, and my club will protect themselves no matter what. I just hope that they find me when I'm still alive.

"Are you going to make my daughter come to us?" Keegan's dad asks me, throwing a bucket of freezing water on me to wake me up.

I yell and sputter until I'm slapped, yes slapped, across the face by the evil man in front of me. "No. I will never do anythin' to get Keegan to come to you. You are no father of hers and I won't let you try to corrupt her more than what you've already done."

"Wrong answer," he says calmly, before motioning to men hiding in the darkness around me.

Instead of coming towards me, the men make their way over to Riley and begin to assault her any way they can again. I hate seeing her go through this, but that's not going to make me give up the love of my life. Instead, I'm going to make sure the attention is turned towards me. I'll make them torture and torment me.

"You scumbags are really that much of a pussy that you have to take your lack of manhood out on a defenseless woman?" I yell out as loud as I can.

My throat is dry, and I know my voice is low and scratchy. I really need a drink, but they give us almost nothing. At this rate, we'll die of dehydration and starvation before anything else. But, once a day we get scraps of mush and some water. Just enough to keep us alive so they can continue to torture us.

I continue to call out obscenities and try to get the men to turn their attention to me. Finally, they stop their assault on her and give me what I want. The six men start pummeling me and beating me until I once again fall into unconscious. My last thoughts as always are Keegan, Kasey, and our twins.

"Rage? Can you hear me?" a soft voice calls to me, almost in a dreamlike state.

"Huh?" I ask, starting to come to.

"Let them come after me Rage. Please save yourself for Keegan and your children."

"Riley?" I ask, confused as to what's going on right now.

"Yeah, it's me."

"I can't do that. You know that."

"Keegan is going to need you. I'll be fine, you need to let me do this for her," Riley pleads with me. "Everything I love has already been ripped away from me. There's not much else they can do to me. Please let me give this to Keegan to show her how much she means to me."

"Keegan wouldn't want you to do this. She knows how much you care about her. She will come back to you, it's just goin' to take some time."

"Let me give this to her. Let me send you home to her so she can be free and happy for once in her life. I've never seen her shine the way she does now."

"How did they even get to you?" I ask, curiosity getting the better of me.

"I went out back to have a smoke. It's not something I do a lot, but I needed one and one of the club girls let me get one from her. The table right by the door is where I sit so I am close to the door. Anyway, two men grabbed me from behind. I didn't hear them coming and I don't know how they got in. As soon as they had me, they put something over my face. I woke up here."

Before much more can be said, the men return to the warehouse and I know our daily torture is about to begin. Only this time, there's a man that I haven't seen before. I'm guessing that the coward before us is Sam. Took him long enough to show his fucking face. I can't wait to get my hands on this mother fucker!

"So, you're the man that has defiled my beautiful betrothed?" he asks me in a whiny voice.

I can't help laughing at the childish quality of his voice when he looks like his shit don't stink. This man is dressed impeccably and not a hair is out of place on his head. I bet he even gets manicures on a regular basis. Sam is the type of man that won't get his hands dirty. No, he'll hire dumb fucks that don't know any better to do his dirty work.

"I'm the man that has a woman, and children on the way. You don't have shit to do with my girl!" I yell, spitting on the man in front of me.

It's petty and I know I'm going to pay for it, but he is a sick fuck and deserves so much more than that. If I could get down from here, I would beat his ass to a pulp and that's with all the pain I'm in, all the abuse I've suffered since I've been here. We can't even tell how much time we've been gone because there's no windows in this room. Riley and I have no clue if it's day or night.

"You think you can defy me and I still won't get what I'm after?" Sam asks. "All I have to do is send a video of the abuse you're both suffering through and she'll cave in an instant."

"That's where you're wrong. She has a whole club behind her and she's not the weak and mild girl that you're lookin' for. Keegan is strong and will stand her ground to protect those she loves. She's not goin' to do anything to put our babies in jeopardy. Think again asshat," I spit out, the pain starting to take me under again.

"We'll see how easily she caves in. Take the video of both of them. Send it to the burner and I'll send it out later today," Sam then walks away, and I see that some men are surrounding Riley. I can't do anything to stop it today though. Darkness is pullin me under again.

Keegan

It's been almost a week since the love of my life was taken from us. Since Kasey lost her daddy. We've had no word from anyone about him. Riley also hasn't been seen around the clubhouse and I can't help the doubt creeping in that she had something to do with this. I really don't want to think this way, but it sure seems to be a coincidence that they're both missing. Well, I was supposed to be the one missing.

Kasey isn't handling this well at all. She won't leave my side, she barely eats or drinks, and none of the other kids can get her to go with them for any reason. Needless to say, Anthony has been sticking close to her and Glock and Melody have been spending time with us too. Whitney and Sami have been trying to get Kasey to come back out of her shell too. Nothing is working and there's no way that any of that is going to happen until Rage comes home. I can't even bring myself to think if something so bad happens to him that he doesn't make it back.

"Mama?" Kasey asks, waking up from our nap.

"Yeah baby," I answer, running my fingers through her hair.

"Is daddy really coming home?"

"Yeah. Daddy will make it back. He has to. Daddy has you and the new babies to live for."

"What if he doesn't?"

"Sweetheart, your daddy will make it home to us," Grim responds from the doorway. "Uncle Grim and every single one of your other uncles are workin' on it day and night."

"Okay unca Grim. We needs daddy," she responds quietly.

Kasey rolls her back to us and I can feel her little body shaking with silent tears. She's trying to be so strong for me, she thinks I need her to be strong. Anthony crawls into the bed on the opposite side and wraps his arms around the little girl. I can hear murmuring and know that he's trying to tell her everything is going to be okay. Until Rage comes home, she won't let the belief in though.

"Melody is comin' in to sit with Kasey for a little bit. We need you in church with us Keegan," Grim tells me.

"I'm not supposed to be in there."

"There's exceptions. This is one of them. We got a video and are waitin' on you to see it."

"I don't think I can watch it," I tell him honestly.

Grim nods in understanding but tells me they want me in there regardless. I can turn my head away or whatever I have to do. The men voted, and they think I need to be a part of this. Especially if Sam tries to call or get in touch with us at all. This way I can be in on whatever game plan is come up with.

Melody knocks on the door a few minutes after Grim leaves and I know it's time for me to make my way to the common room. They're all waiting in there for me. My body is killing me, and my feet feel like lead weights as I get out of bed and make my way towards the common room. This is the last thing I want to do and it's draining all parts of me.

"Guys!" Grim calls out. "Church!"

Grim and Pops stand on either side of me and lead me into the room they meet. After taking his seat at the table, Grim motions for me to sit next to him in Joker's spot. I don't want to take his seat, but Joker holds the chair out for me and I sit down. Standing behind me,

Joker offers a silent support while Pops takes my hand. Tank goes to the computer and pulls up the email that was sent to them. Before he plays the video, there's a note.

Keegan,

You have greatly disappointed me. Instead of coming home and taking your rightful place by my side, you have chosen to be defiled by a heathen. Now, everything that happens is on you. I hope that you can live with yourself. It's only going to get worse the longer it takes for you to turn yourself over to me.

Your Loving Man,

Sam

The tears are already streaming down my face as I look around the table. I know what I have to do, and no one here is going to let me do it. Pops holds my hand tighter like he can feel what's going through my head right now. Tank takes a few minutes before he presses the button to play the video. The first thing we see is Riley hanging from the rafters in a roof. She's surrounded by men and they are violating her in the worst way. There's no need for me to say a word, a garbage can is placed in front of me as I throw up what little is in my stomach.

Next, we see Rage in the same position. He's being attacked by the same men that just beat and raped Riley. They aren't holding back, and the tears are flowing freely down my face. There are various shades of purples and blacks on his body that we can see. Both of his eyes are swollen shut, his face is swollen period, just looking you can see at least one arm is badly broken, and that's just from taking him in quickly. I can't watch and Pops and Joker sense this.

Before I know it, both men are surrounding me so I don't have to watch. Pops is pulling my face into his neck to shield me further, and Tank has turned all sound off, so I don't have to hear the beating my man is getting right now. All because they want me. I need to turn myself over to them. One way or another this is what I have to do.

Not only is my heart breaking for my man, it's breaking for Riley. I let the fact that she was approached by them delude me into believing she had something to do with her missing. That she allowed them to get to her again and trap her into helping them. The pain and anguish written on her once beautiful face will forever be etched into my memory. When she gets back, I will do whatever I have to in order to help her heal. Not just physically but emotionally too.

"That's enough Tank. There's a number to call, so I think we should call it now," Grim tells everyone in the room.

I hear him dialing a phone before placing it on speaker and setting it on the table in front of him. It rings so long that I almost think no one is going to answer it. That they're just going to play further games with us. With me. Trying to get inside my head more than what they have already with sending the video.

"I see you received my email. Now, let's get down to negotiations," I hear Sam's voice through the phone. It makes my skin crawl and I want to scream and yell.

"We did. You think that by havin' our family in your possession will make us want to work with you at all?" Grim asks.

"You're going to work with me and give me what I want. Or, you're going to start receiving little pieces in the mail. Not just of your so-called brother either. Riley is still a feisty little bitch and is slowly learning her place. I have no use for her, so she can suffer the same fate," Sam tells us.

"What do you think is goin' to happen here?" Grim asks, folding his arms on the table in front of him.

"You're going to hand my woman over to me and I'll let you know where you can find the scum that I have in my possession now."

"That's not goin' to work for us. If you want Keegan, then you can meet us with Riley and Rage. If you can't see fit to do that, then I can't see any reason to bring Keegan to you," Grim responds, staring at me to gauge my reaction.

"And you think that I'm really going to meet with you. I have people that do that for me."

"I know you do. I also know that you'll be somewhere close by watchin' the exchange too. See, bein' a cocky fuckwad like yourself, you're goin' to want to watch everythin'. You're just not man enough to get your hands dirty. You don't have the balls to face me head on and get the one thing that you want because she managed to elude you for so long."

"Do you really think that's going to make me meet you, Grim? You have to be smarter than that," Sam responds, letting his cocky side out more and more.

"I know it's goin' to. You can't stand to have someone, even me, think that you're not a man. That you can't handle your own business."

Sam goes quiet for so long that I almost think he's hung up. He'll only let someone push him for so long before he lets his rage and cockiness take over. Finally, we hear shuffling on the other end of the line and Sam's voice again.

"Fine. I will meet you. But, it will just be you and Keegan. On my end, it will be myself and her dad. We'll have what you want. I'm warning you now, if you try to play any games, she'll be dead before any of you can blink. I'll even let you choose where and when we meet. Does that satisfy you?"

"Yes, it does. We'll meet in thirty minutes. There's an old turn off on the outskirts of town. You know where I'm talking about?"

"I do."

"Thirty minutes. The same goes for you Sam. If you try to pull anythin', I will shoot first and ask questions later."

Grim hangs up and I let my head fall back. I'm not sure exactly what's going through everyone's head right now. Sam is a dangerous man and they really don't know who they're dealing with. He'll have the place surrounded.

"Don't worry Keegan," Cage tells me. "We've already got our guys there. Grim knew this would happen. We've dealt with his type before."

"No, you really haven't. He's dispatching his guys as we speak. They'll let him know you already have people there."

"Not when they can't speak," Joker responds. "We have two of the best snipers there already on opposite sides. Slim and his crew are spaced out all over the place. They wouldn't even tell us where they were goin' to be."

"If you really think that you know what you're doing, I'll go along with whatever is going to get them back. If you have to let me go with them to save Rage, please let them take me," I plead with everyone in the room. "You need to get him back to our girl. I'll be fine. He's not going to hurt me too bad."

"No happenin' firefly," Pops explodes. "Trust in us. We'll be bringin' you all home."

We're finally at the meeting spot and the nerves are running rampant through my body. There's so many things that can go wrong right now. Rage and Riley don't need to be hurt any more than they already have at the sadistic hands of Sam and my father. I know it wasn't them personally that did these things to them, but they had a hand in it. They gave the orders to rape and brutally beat my best friend, to brutally attack a man that was bound and couldn't fight back.

"I hope you guys are right," I say, letting the nerves come out.

"I know your worried firefly," Grim begins. "We've already got eyes on you, his men have already been taken care of, and Killer already has Sam and your dad in his scope. We got this."

"Just know that I'm okay if you have to let me go," I tell him honestly.

Before anything else can be said, a car pulls up. The windows are tinted and there's no way to see who's inside. Please, let my man and sister from another mister be in there, I silently beg. Three doors open, and I can see two bodies hit the ground. Apparently, one of the men is sitting in the back and just pushed Rage and Riley out the doors and to the ground. I can hear their grunts and groans from where I stand, and I lean to the side to throw up. How much more can these two people take before their bodies give up completely?

Grim puts his hand on my back and tries to offer comfort and reassurance. It's not working but I appreciate the gesture nonetheless. I see Sam step out as soon as Grim touches me and I know he's going to have something smart to say about it. This is probably also going to result in something else happening to the two people I care about most in the world. Fuck!

"I see you let anyone and everyone touch you these days," Sam begins. "I'm beginning to wonder if I even want you to come with me. Maybe this trade won't happen after all."

I scream out uncontrollably. There's no way these two can withstand any more. They need to be taken to a hospital and get better. Kasey needs her dad and I know that Riley will be there for her and Rage in my absence. Hopefully I'll be able to send the twins to their dad. No matter what anyone says, I need to do whatever has to be done to get these two men away from my family.

"Stop!" I shout out. "Please leave them alone!"

"Like I said, you'll let anyone touch you these days. Now, I want you to start walking towards me and I'll make sure no one touches the two on the ground. If anything is attempted, there's already a gun trained on her," Sam calls out.

Grim nods his head at me to start slowly moving forward. I move as slow as I dare before Sam starts screaming at me to move my fat ass. There's no way I can move any faster though when I see Rage trying his hardest to push himself off the ground and make his way to me. His eyes are burning holes through me, he's silently pleading with me to turn around and make my way back to Grim. I can't do that though. There's a plan in place and I need to do this in order for the plan to happen.

Without letting on, I see Slim and another man sneaking up behind the car that Sam drove here. For bigger men, they truly are silent on their feet. I get a few more steps in and my dad hit's the ground. I already know that they were going to try something and whoever just pulled the trigger must have seen him making a move none of us on the ground could witness.

Sam spins around and takes his eyes off me as Grim sprints forward to get me back in his possession and away from Sam. The two men coming around the car grab Sam before he knows what hit him. They take him to the ground and secure his legs and arms behind him. A van comes flying up the dead-end road, stirring up all sorts of dirt and debris in it's haste to stop and get the man I've been running from for years loaded up.

As soon as Grim lets me go, I'm at Rage's side. He's barely moving, and I know that he's in so much pain right now. There's blood flowing from several open wounds and I can't find a single part of his skin that doesn't have bruising on it. They've cut his clothes off him so all he's wearing right now are a pair of boxers. I'm surprised they left him in those.

Looking over, I see Gage leaning over Riley. He's trying to cover as much of her exposed skin as he possibly can. From the look in his eyes, he doesn't want anyone else to see her. Where they at least left Rage in his boxers, Riley is wearing nothing. One of the guys hands Gage a shirt from somewhere and he gently lays it over her battered body.

"Can someone please get them some help?" I cry out, getting as close to Rage as I possibly can. "We need to get them to the hospital!"

Grim leans down next to me and I see the phone already to his ear. He's giving someone our location and I can only hope that it's the paramedics. I'll take the blame for my dad being dead, I'll spend the rest of my life in prison if I have to. At this point, the only thing I can think of is making sure that they get the help they need immediately.

"They'll be here soon Keegan," Grim tells me.

I'm whispering to Rage how much I love him, and we need him to come home. I want nothing more than to pull him in my arms, but I can't do that. There's too many injuries and I don't want to make anything worse. Without knowing the extent, I leave him where he's lying and comfort him the best I can. Unfortunately, I'm not sure how much he hears as he passes out. Screaming once again, I pray that he's just blacked out and not leaving us.

My sole focus is on Rage and I don't hear anything around me. When a paramedic touches my shoulder, I scream. "Ma'am, we need you to move so we can get started on him."

I quickly move out of the way so that I'm not wasting time. Another group of paramedics are surrounding Riley and Gage isn't moving very far away from her. It's all I can do to get as far away from Rage as I am. Grim tells the paramedics that I'm riding with him and his tone leaves no room for argument. So, within a matter of minutes, we're loading up in the ambulances and making our way to the hospital.

Chapter Nine

Rage

I'VE BEEN SURROUNDED BY darkness for so long. In the distance I can hear noises and what sounds like someone talking to me, but I can't make myself leave the darkness. The few times that I've come close, my body hurts so bad, I quickly retreat.

I'm not sure if my mind is playing tricks on me or not, but I swear I keep seeing my mom. Rationally, I know that she's no longer with us, but my mind doesn't seem to know that. Every time I see her, she gets closer and closer, I can hear her speaking clearer than the last time. Maybe this means that I'm getting ready to leave this world behind.

"Son, you can't leave. You have to make yourself wake up and deal with the pain," she tells me.

"I can't."

"You can, and you will. Kasey needs you. They all need you. Keegan and the babies on the way need you to be there for them. I'll always be by your side, but they need you now. Go to them!"

With a painful jolt, I begin to wake up and open my eyes. The most beautiful sight greets me as I slightly turn my head to the side. Keegan is laying her head next to me and I can see the tears shimmering on her pale skin, the dark circles under her eyes, and the pain lingering in her frown. One of her dainty hands are holding mine so I try to move my fingers on that hand.

"Rage?" she asks, quickly lifting her head and looking at me.

My throat is so dry and scratchy that I don't even try to talk yet. I look at the water sitting on the stand at the end of my bed and she follows my eyes. Before she can stand to get it for me, I see Grim step forward and pour me water. He walks around the side of the bed and holds the straw so that I don't really have to move in order to take a small sip of water. I've seen enough to know that no matter how much I want to, I can't gulp down the water. I have to take small sips. After a minute I feel like I can talk a little even though my throat is still killing me.

"Firefly, I love you," I tell her.

"I love you too baby. I was so scared. Kasey is here, she's waiting to see you."

"Get our daughter," I tell her so that I can talk to Grim for a second before doctors and everyone else invades my room. "You get them?"

"Waitin' on you brother. He's on ice until you come home and are good enough to dish out the pain. Let that rage build up so you can unleash it where it belongs."

I give a slight nod to let him know I understand what he's telling me. Within seconds, my girls enter the room followed by the doctor. He does his exam as Kasey sit's in Keegan's lap. She's talking a mile a minute about how much she loves me and missed me. Things that we need to do when I come home. The movement she's felt on Keegan's stomach from the babies. I love this little girl to death and I'm so happy that she's here right now. I need my girls around me.

I've been in the hospital for another week and a half since waking up. Today is the day that I finally get to go home and I'm more than ready to get the fuck out of here. Keegan has been here the entire time. The girls brought her clothes and stuff so that she could shower here. Skylar has been bringing food to us too. At first, the doctor didn't like the idea, but Skylar was very persistent. So, I've been eating her cooking and had my girls here with me every day. The nights are when Keegan and I talk and laugh, we plan for the future, and everything else.

"You ready to go sunshine?" Joker asks, coming in my room.

"Fuck yeah," I tell him, sitting up on the bed so that Keegan can finish putting my shirt on me.

She said she wanted to do this for me, and what man is going to tell their old lady they can't do something as simple as help them get dressed? I'll take my firefly's hands on me in any way possible. I'm so lost in my own little world that I don't notice her getting ready to put my boots on until I see Joker making his way over to us. He's not going to let her get down and put my boots on me, he'll do it himself.

"I can do this, ya know?" she asks, letting her sass shine through.

"I know you can firefly. But, I can do it too. Let me do this for my brother. Please?" he asks, trying to appeal to her softer side.

"I guess. I'll go make sure everything is packed up."

Once my girl is out of the room, I let Joker know that I'm ready to get my hands dirty. He tells me to wait on the doctor and see what he has to say before we make any plans for retribution to begin when we get to the clubhouse. I get where he's coming from, but I've sat in this bed for a week with my mind coming up with multiple ways to torture this motherfucker. Not only for what he wanted to do to my girl, but for what happened to Riley and myself when he took us. Not to mention what my little peanut went through while I was missing and since I've been in the hospital. Kasey cries every night she has to leave us behind. That ends today though, now I need to get my hands dirty and take out the rage that has been building up since I met my firefly.

"I think I got everything baby," Keegan tells me, coming back to the hospital bed I'm sitting on.

"Okay. Looks like we're just waitin' on the doc to show up."

"I can go get him," Joker says, heading for the door.

I'm sure he's as ready to leave this place as I am. And he hasn't been the one stuck in this bed. He has been here every day though; all my brothers have. Joker has stayed the longest though every single day. I don't know why, but I'll never be able to repay him for the support he's shown Keegan and me.

Keegan

Rage has been home for a few days and he's getting restless. The doctor wants him to take it easy and that's not in his vocabulary. About the only good thing is that we're in our home and not in the room at the clubhouse. So, when he gets moody and irritable, I just leave the bedroom and start working on another room in the house.

The guys have been coming over to see him and try to keep him in a good mood, but it doesn't always work out that way. Most of the time, they end up arguing with him about whatever he has in his mind to do. At this point, I've given up on trying to guess what he's trying to do. But, the doctor wants him to rest for at least a few days before he gets up and starts moving around. Today is day number three and he's ready to go.

"Hey firefly," Wood says, coming in. "How are things today with him?"

"Do you really need to ask? I'm cleaning the floor on my hands and knees, so I have an excuse to be away from him."

"Well, maybe I'll get him away from the house for a while today. That sound good?"

"Yes!" I practically scream. "Let me tell him to shower and get dressed."

With how big I've gotten, there's no way I can run down the hall to the bedroom. But, I do waddle as fast as my ass will go. I'm definitely moving much slower these days and I'm not liking it at all. I feel like a beached whale and I can't wait for the next three months to go by, so we can meet our little ones.

"Rage, get up and in the shower. I'll get your clothes while you're washing up," I tell him, entering the bedroom to see him mindlessly flipping through the stations on the tv.

"What are you talkin' about?" he asks, not bothering to look at me.

"Wood is taking you out. Get ready to go. Now!"

Rage takes a few minutes to look at me and the realization that he's been an ass with how moody he's been sets in. I can tell the exact moment he understands why I want him out of the house so bad. He gets out of bed and instead of making his way over to the bathroom, he walks over to me.

"I'm sorry baby. I know I've been an ass the last few days. I'm used to bein' up and movin' around whenever I want to. This shit is killin' me. But, I know I need reign it in."

"I love you, Rage. But if you ever get laid up again, you're staying in the clubhouse. You're a jackass when you can't do anything."

Rage chuckles as he walks into the bathroom. I get his clothes for him so we can get him out of the house sooner rather than later. Kasey comes in and I tell her that daddy is leaving for a little bit, so we're going to bake and start making dinner. She gets excited and runs in to wash her hands.

Once Rage is out of the shower, I walk with him to the door and give him a kiss. Kasey gives Rage a hug and kiss before he turns and walk out the door. Wood gives us a grin and wink over his shoulder as he leads my man towards the clubhouse. Finally, some peace without the tension of a moody asshole in the house.

As soon as we got the brownies and cookies out of the oven, I asked Kasey if she wanted to go see Riley for a little bit. I haven't been able to get to the clubhouse to see her, but the other girls have told me she hasn't really moved from her bed. They check on her and make sure that her bandages and stuff are clean and changed on a regular basis. I'm going to have to be the one to talk to her and get her up and moving. It's going to take me to get her to go see someone so that she can start healing and we can get back to where we were before all this shit happened.

Bailey and Skylar take Kasey as soon as we walk through the door. Kasey will get her chance to see Riley, but I need some time alone with her first. I need to give her some tough love so that she at least gets up out of the bed. Melody also hands me a card that has the name for a counselor on it. She tells me quietly that several of them have used her and she's amazing. If that's the case, I know the first thing we're doing.

"Riley, I'm coming in whether you like it or not," I say, opening the door.

The blinds are shut tight and it's so dark in her room. This is not going to do at all. So, I open all the curtains and see her cover her face with a pillow. Not happening on my watch. Riley has done similar things to me when I needed it and I have no problem reminding her of those times.

"Let's go!" I tell her. "It's time to get out of this bed and start healing. I'm going to help you and be by your side the way you've been by side more times than I can count."

"Keegan, you don't need to do this to make yourself feel better," she mutters under the pillow.

"I'm not doing this to make myself feel better. I'm doing this to make you feel better," I tell her, wrenching the pillow from her hands and tossing it on the floor. "Now, get your ass in the shower and we're going to my house, so you can eat and hang out with Kasey and I."

"I don't want to."

"I don't give a fuck! Don't make my fat, pregnant ass try to pick your skinny ass up."

Riley looks up at me to see how serious I am. Once she sees the determination on my face, she knows she has no choice in the matter. I grab her clothes and lead the way to the bathroom she has in her room. I'm not giving her any excuse, so I even turn on the water and get it to the temperature I know she likes. As soon as she steps foot in the bathroom, I stand in front of the closed door, so she can't get out and wait for her to get in. Then I move to sit on the toilet and keep her company while she washes up and lets the hot water run over her body. I bet it's soothing her muscles with the way she's just standing there letting the water cascade over her.

"You don't have to sit in here with me," she says.

"I know I don't. But you need to hear some things and there's no time like the present," I begin. "First and foremost, I'm sorry that I ever doubted you. You've never given me any reason to believe that you were truly going to work with my dad and the motherfucker that wanted to kidnap me. Can you forgive me?"

"There's nothing to forgive. I should've told you a long time ago."

"Now, I'm sorry that you got kidnapped and abused the way you did because of me."

"It wasn't because of you," she interrupts me. "It's because I didn't follow his orders and I've been looking into something. Keegan, I had a baby after you took off. The baby is no part of Sam, but he found out and managed to take my little girl out of the hospital before I knew what was happening. She's about to turn one and I have no clue what she even looks like. I want her back so bad and he's threatened me, so I haven't looked real close until I got here. I was going to talk to Gage about helping me find her."

"Why didn't you tell me?" I ask, astonishment lacing my voice.

"I didn't know how to tell you."

"The next thing we need to talk about is getting you in to talk to someone. I saw a little bit of what they did to you Riley and I'm so sorry."

"I already planned on finding someone. Please don't pity me. I don't want that from you. You're my sister and I just need you to have my back and work our way back to getting where we were."

"I don't pity you. I think that you're one of the strongest people I know, and I just want to help you get even stronger."

"I'm ready to get out. So, dinner at your house tonight?" she asks me, climbing into the towel I'm holding for her.

"Yeah. You don't really have a choice in the matter."

"Rage won't care?"

"I don't really care if he likes it or not. He's been a moody asshole the last few days."

Riley laughs at my description of Rage. I've missed talking like this with her, acting like there's nothing wrong in our private little world. Today, we start getting back to that. So, we head over to my house with Kasey, blare the music, dance around the kitchen while making dinner. I'm not doing all that much dancing, but we're all having so much fun it doesn't really matter.

This is how Rage finds us as he walks through the door with Wood and Gage a few hours later. He watches us for a few minutes before making his way over to me. There's a smile on his face and I can once again she the love shining from his eyes. Our life is finally getting back on track and I couldn't be happier.

Chapter Ten

Rage

THE LAST FEW DAYS I'VE BEEN in to see Sam. He's tied to the rafters in one of the rooms in the basement just like Riley and I were tied up. Someone has stripped him completely and I know the first thing I'm going to do to him when I get the go ahead from Grim. Hopefully it's soon because I'm getting itchy to release this pent-up aggression.

"Rage, are you ready to finally get your hands on this scumbag?" Grim asks, walking in the door behind me.

"I'm more than ready. There's so much I need to do to him for Keegan, Riley, myself, and more importantly my daughter."

"Let me get the guys in here and you can give him your worst."

Within a few minutes, every member we can possibly fit in this room is standing behind me. Tank has brought in an assortment of tools and torture devices for me to use. I turn to Blade for my first mission though.

"Blade, I need your dullest one man," I let him know, holding out my hand to see what he's going to hand me.

"Here you go. Been savin' this one for a special occasion. This one seems like the perfect one."

I take the blade that he's just handed me, and I move closer to Sam. He's going to scream like a little bitch. I'm not going to let him pass out. As soon as he does, we'll wake him back up. This twatwaffle is going to feel every ounce of pain I want to inflict on him.

"So, you never seem to get your hands dirty. Can you Sam?" I begin. "And I know my President flat out told you that you didn't have any balls. So, let's make that a reality."

Without another word, I begin to separate his balls from his body. Every single man in this room is cringing and groaning from watching what I'm doing. A few actually look like they might get sick. Sam is screaming like the bitch he is. I'm not giving him a break though. As soon as he starts to pass out, I stop until he's alert and start again.

I made sure that there was a doctor that does work for the club every now and then present so that Sam wouldn't die before I was done with him. Nodding to him after a minute, I want him to stop the bleeding as much as possible, so he doesn't die from blood loss when there's so much more pain for him to feel. I'm not playing with this fucker and all the mental torture my girl suffered at his hands. She had to run and hide for most of her life because of him. Then to witness what the douche canoe ordered to be done to Riley and her child. I will be finding out where her son or daughter is. Once Keegan finds out about it, she'll make sure that as many people as possible help find the missing child.

Using the same blade, I begin to slice tiny cuts all over his body. Riley was cut with huge blades all over her body. Sam needs to feel what she felt. As soon as I think that he's got enough cuts in his skin, I take a handful of salt and rub it into as many as I can. Screams and moans rip from Sam no matter how hard he tries to act tough and hold it in.

"I need a small break," I announce. "Anyone else want a go at him?"

Glock and Tank both step up. I'll stay in the room, but I need to sit down for a second. I'm still in pain and this is taking more out of me than what I thought it would. Blade and Cage stand next to me in case I need help. Closing my eyes, I think of more ways I can torture this man. I'm listening to the sounds of Glock, Tank, and whoever else getting their hit's in while they can. There are so many things I want to do to him, but there's not going to be enough time to do them all. So, I'll do what I can in the little amount of time I'm given.

"Rage, we might have a problem," a prospect says, coming in the room we're in.

"What's that?" I ask, puzzled.

"Keegan wants to come get a hit or two in."

I look around the room at my brothers. Normally we wouldn't even consider doing something like this. However, after the time and pain my girl has endured, I'm going to give her this. After nodding at the prospect, I stand so that I can be the first-person firefly sees. She cautiously enters the room and finds me immediately. I nod to her and hold my hand out. After she takes my hand, I pull her into my body so she can't see past me.

"We've already had fun with him firefly. You need to prepare yourself for what you see. It's not pretty," I warn her.

"I know. It's nothing that he doesn't deserve. I'm just sorry that my dad isn't feeling the same pain he is."

Looking into her eyes, I try to gauge what's going through her mind right now. There's no hesitation, no fear, nothing that's going to make me change my mind right now. The only things I see are pure hatred, disgust, and pain for whatever she has learned happened to Riley and myself. I ask if she's ready and there's no hesitation before she nods.

Stepping to the side, I watch her reaction as she takes in Sam's appearance for the first time. My girl is strong as fuck as she takes step after step towards him. I see her grab a hammer on her way over to him and I'm intrigued as to what she has going through her mind right now. We don't have to wait long though.

"How dare you prey on young girls, you sick fuck!" she yells. "You will *never* touch another girl again!"

Before any of us can do anything, Keegan starts hitting Sam anywhere she can with the hammer in her hand. I let her go until I can see her getting tired. Then I know that she's had enough, and I need to stop her. As I pull her into my arms, I see the tears flowing down her face and the pain etched in her eyes. My girl has had enough and I'm going to take her home now. These motherfuckers can finish him off. I want to be the one to end him, but Keegan needs me more right now.

"Pres, I'm out. My girl needs me more than endin' this cocksucker. Make him fuckin' pay!" I grit out before making my way towards the door.

"You got it brother. Anythin' in mind you want done to him?" Grim asks me.

"Yeah. I think he needs to burn for the pain he caused all those other little girls," I tell him, motioning my head towards the torch sitting on the bench where I left it. "And check his back for tattoos. There's no way he's doin' this shit alone."

"Got it. Get firefly home and we'll let you know when it's done."

Once we're out the door, Keegan lets go of me and looks me in the eyes. She's searching for something and no matter what I do, she'll find what she's looking for. Keegan is the only person I know that can read me and know exactly what I'm thinking and feeling without me letting on to anything.

"Go back in there babe," she tells me. "I know you want to be the one to end him. Finish it for me so I know without a doubt that it's done."

"No…" I start to say.

"Please. Do it for me. I need to know that he's dead and never going to hurt another person as long as we live. That there's never going to be a chance for him to come after our daughter. You will make sure that doesn't happen. Go back in there. I'll go with the other girls and wait for you to get done. I'll be fine."

My girl had to bring up the one thing guaranteed to make me go back in that room. No motherfucker will ever get his dirty, grimy hands on our daughter. I will gut a cocksucker before that happens. Kissing Keegan, I walk back in the room to the screams of Sam. Blade and Pops are working him over and I can just imagine what they're doing to him.

"What's up?" Grim asks me.

"Keegan wants me to be the one to finish him off. She knows that I'll make sure this motherfucker won't ever be able to touch our daughter."

"Step in when you want to then," Grim tells me.

I remove my cut and shirt before letting Pops and Blade know that I'll be taking back over. Walking around the asshole that has haunted my girl's dreams for way to long, I think about what I want to do to him next. Pausing at his back, I see that he does in fact have ink. It's small and what the Soulless Bastards used to wear when they were still around. I call attention to this and the men all move in closer to him. Especially Cage, Joker, and Grim.

"Looks like we didn't get all of them," Grim says, picking up a bottle of alcohol before walking to his back.

Pointing out the small tattoo, I watch as my President pours a liberal amount of alcohol over Sam's back. Knowing what comes next, I make sure to light the torch where Sam can see. It doesn't take a rocket scientist to know what we're going to do. Sam starts moving around as much as he can to try to get as far away from me as he can. Honestly, he can't go very far. We made sure of that.

Walking around Sam, I let the torch get closer and closer to his body. There's no way he can't feel the heat from it. Sam is really starting to squirm now. I'm not one to feel pain for those that like to torture and beat on others. When it comes to Sam, I really have nothing but hatred and rage to feel. Not only has he preyed on little girls, but he's been tracking and trying to get my girl since she was little.

Putting the torch to his body, I watch the flames take off from the alcohol Grim poured on his body. The flames go down his back. I stand there mesmerized as I listen to his screams. The guys are standing there watching right along with me. Especially those involved personally with what happened with the Soulless Bastards. They fucked with Skylar and Bailey at one point or another.

After what seems like forever, we douse the flames just after Sam's screams have faded. I'm not sure if he passed out from the pain or if he's dead. I nod my head at the doc and he checks him. It takes him a minute, but he tells us he can feel a pulse very faintly. I'm not going to let him die like this though. So, I pull my gun and point it at his head. I'm covered in splatter, but it's worth it to be able to tell my girl that he's finally gone and has nothing to worry about anymore.

Before going to get cleaned up, I text Bailey to make sure my girl was okay. Once I got the response, I ran up to shower in Cage and Joker's room so that neither one of my girls would see me looking the way I did. That's something I don't ever want to have to explain to our daughter. And, I don't need Keegan to see me covered in Sam's blood. It's bad enough that she was down there and got her hands dirty. My only concern is that I'll be able to tell her that it's over with. Now, we just need to look into what role he played with the Soulless Bastards and how many more there are out there.

Finally cleaned up, I go in search of my girls. I need the calm that they bring me and the peace that I find in their arms. Kasey and Keegan are sitting on one of the couches in the main room, talking about something. My daughter is the first one to notice me and I see her push off the couch and run towards me. I brace myself to catch her flying body as she launches herself at me. Keegan just remains seated, watching the two of us. I can't say that I blame her as it's getting harder and harder for her to move around.

After giving my daughter hugs and kisses, I make my way over to Keegan. Sitting down next to her, I whisper that she no longer has anything to worry about. Firefly's entire body sags in relief as I relay the information to her. She closes her eyes and I can see a few tears slipping out. This time, I know they're tears of so many different emotions and there's nothing I can really do except for be there for the love of my life.

Chapter Eleven

Riley

THIS MORNING THE GIRLS CAME pounding on my door. I guess they decided to have a baby shower and bridal shower all rolled into one for Keegan. There's no way in hell I'm missing this. So, I got ready to go and we went shopping.

"What are you getting for her, Riley?" Skylar asks me.

"I'm getting a little bit of everything. The things I wish I got to use on my baby girl," I respond without thinking.

"Did you lose a child?" she asks.

"In a way."

Skylar thankfully lets the subject drop as I begin to load my cart with things. I grab a few blankets, bottles, pajamas, onesies, diapers and wipes, along with little bottles of everything they'll need to wash the babies and make them smell amazing. Damn I wish I got to smell that with my daughter. I can't let myself go down that road though. Not today. When I'm alone later on, I can think about the what-ifs and where my little peanut is. That's all I have. I didn't even get a chance to see her after I had her.

"When we're done here, we're going back to the adult store for some bridal shower gifts. Keegan better have a good sense of humor!" Bailey tells us all.

I glance over at Darcy and see her face turning a few shades of red. We had to sneak her here because Keegan doesn't know what the girls planned for her. They want to surprise her after the hell she's been through with Rage and I being kidnapped and because she's at the point in her pregnancy that she's absolutely miserable. Still, she's trying to do everything for everyone around her. Me included.

"Riley, I know that we don't know one another," Darcy says coming up to me. "But, I'd like to change that. I know there's a history between you and Riley and I'm here for you whenever you need me."

"Thank you, Darcy. That means a lot to me. I'm not sure that I'm staying in the area though. Now that the threat is gone, I can leave here and start to rebuild my life. Figure out who I'm meant to be."

"What were you doing before you came here?" she asks me, truly wanting to get to know me.

"I was a hair dresser. I did it all. Hair, manicures, pedicures, and I was thinking about going to school for massages as well."

"Are you shitting me?" she asks, incredulous. "I need a stylist at my salon. Would you be willing to move to Dander Falls and work for me?"

"You don't know anything about my work. How can you offer me a job?" I ask, not wanting to believe a job just landed in my lap.

"I don't mean to interrupt, but I need a cut and color done. I'd be willing to be a guinea pig," Maddie says, looking between the two of us.

"That works for me if you want to do it," Darcy says, looking hopeful.

"I can do it. What color are you thinking?"

"I want to go dark blond again. That's usually what Darcy does for me. I need it done again."

We make arrangements for me to do Maddie's hair tomorrow afternoon. Darcy wasn't planning on spending the night, but now she's going to. I guess this means that eventually the guys will be showing up. The two men that follow her around are never far behind her. I bet they're pissed they haven't figured out where she is already.

Keegan

I'm not sure what the girls are planning, but I know them good enough to know that they're up to something. This morning they all left bright and early. Now, Rage and Kasey are acting strange. I'm so uncomfortable that I can't even pretend to care though. It seems like overnight I blew up to the size of a small house. With having almost three months left in this pregnancy, I'm sure that I'll be the size of a house with garage by the time the twins get here.

Since everyone left the house, I decide to take a warm bath. It's not something I get to do very often and I'm going to take full advantage of an empty house while I can. Once the twins get here, it will be nonstop going all the time. If I'm not with them, I'll be with Kasey so that she's not feeling some kind of way. We don't want her to feel left out or unwanted at all.

Just as I'm going to get in the tub, there's a knocking on the door. Sighing, I turn the water off and put my robe back on, so I can go see who's interrupting my quiet time. Before I open the door, I check the peephole to see who it is. Rage would split a gasket if I didn't check it first. That's how bad things happen.

"What's up Riley?" I ask, opening the door wide.

"Wanted to come see you. They're cleaning my room and I need some place to go for a half hour. Can I chill out? Or do you want me to go somewhere else?"

"No, you're good. I was just going to hop in a bath. I'll take a shower instead. Make yourself at home."

I waddle back in to the bathroom and turn the shower on. So much for the relaxing bath. But, Riley and I are finally getting back on track and I'm going to make sure we stay that way. So, as quick as I can, I wash up and throw a dress on. Dresses are pretty much all I can wear right now.

"Why did they decide to clean your room today?" I ask, making my way back out in the living room.

"I don't know. I think they said something about painting it when I leave."

"What do you mean, 'when you leave'?" I ask, sitting down on the opposite side of the sectional.

"I'm not staying here forever Keegan. You have your life here and I need to find my life now. I need to find my place like you did. Darcy is actually going to possibly give me a chance to work in her salon."

"That's great!" I tell her, genuinely happy that she's making moves to gain her life back.

"I'm going to do Maddie's hair tomorrow to see what she thinks. Then, Darcy will decide if I get a spot in her salon."

"I know you'll get it. I remember you doing my hair all the time before I left. You saved me money I didn't have on haircuts."

We sit and talk for a little bit longer before Riley asks me to walk back over to the clubhouse with her. I can understand why she's hesitant to walk outside alone. I'd probably be the same way as her. Besides, I need to get some exercise. Walking shouldn't hurt me, and I can rest at the clubhouse for a little bit before I make my way back over here. So, I send a message to Rage letting him know what I'm doing before we head out.

I've been sitting here for a few minutes, waiting to get the energy to walk back to the house. Just as I'm going to get up, Kasey comes running up to me. She's bouncing up and down and excited about something. I'm not sure what has her in such a tizzy, but I'm about to find out I guess.

"Mama, you gots to come with me," she tells me, bouncing on her little feet.

"Kasey, calm down sweet pea. She'll get up when she can," Rage says, coming over to help me.

"I knows. But I'm so excited!"

"What's going on Rage?" I ask, my curiosity getting the better of me.

"I'm sworn to secrecy."

Rage walks me into the game room before stepping back and letting me go in the room alone. As soon as I look around, I know why he's not coming in with me. The girls have the room decorated in pinks and blues with balloons, streamers, and banners. The plates, cups, and silverware are also in blues in and pinks. Kasey is standing by the table and I can see the excitement shining from her eyes as she stands before the table loaded down with gifts.

"Mama, looks at all the stuff for the babies. They gots lots of gifts."

"Yes, they do" I reply, the tears forming as I waddle farther into the room. "I can't believe you all put this together for us. Thank you so much!"

"You're part of the club firefly. You're all a part of the family," Bailey tells me, wrapping me in a hug.

"Now, it's time to play some games. Then we'll eat the food the guys are cooking. After that, we'll open gifts so that the kids can leave, and we'll finish the party off," Skylar tells me.

"What do you mean?"

"The other part is a bridal shower hun."

"Wow! You guys have blown me away," I tell everyone. "Thank you so much. I truly needed this today."

Everyone gathers around, and Bailey starts the games. We're laughing so hard that a few times I have to make my way to the bathroom in fear of peeing my pants. I've been slowly sliding into a funk and I didn't know how to tell anyone. Including Rage. This is helping pull me right back out. I still can't do what I want to do with how big I'm getting, but I'll be back to normal soon. I have to keep reminding myself of that.

Bailey even got some cute prizes for the girls that won the games. At one point she pulled a prospect in to clean up some of the debris from the games and I thought he was going to run for the hills at some of the conversations going on around him. Skylar and Darcy were talking about childbirth and the poor guy turned as white as a sheet. I don't think he'll be thinking about having kids anytime soon.

"Are you doing okay?" Riley asks me.

"Yeah. I'm a little tired, but I'm okay."

"Well, how about we have Reagan, Kasey, Zoey, and the rest of the girls help you open the gifts for the baby shower portion of the day?" Bailey asks.

"That would be a tremendous help," I answer them.

"Alright, who wants to help Keegan open the presents for the babies?" Bailey asks the kids.

All of the little girls shout and jump up before running over to me. They're so excited and it's contagious as I find myself catching my second wind. Or maybe it's the third or fourth one for the day. So, we get busy opening the presents while one of the girls writes down who the gift was from and what it was. When I get to Riley's gift, I can feel the love and care that she had when she picked out each item. Knowing what I know about her having a baby out there somewhere, my heart breaks more and more. We have to get her baby back for her. One way or another I will do what I have to in order to find her.

I look at the mound of gifts that have been opened and my tears start again. We have been given everything that a baby could want times two. There's blankets, pacifiers, toys, diapers, wipes, and so much more. The only thing we don't have is something from Pops. He gave us a card with a gift card in it along with a note that the rest of our gift will be delivered in the next two weeks or so. I can't imagine what it's going to be, but I think I have an idea. Skylar and Bailey have talked about cribs and stuff. So, I'm wondering if he had a nursery set made for us. Looking over at Bailey, I see her nod her head at me. She's silently letting me know that my train of thought is right. Pops has had us cribs and things for the nursery made. It touches my heart to know that he considers us family enough to do this for Rage and I.

Everything has been opened for the babies, the guys have taken it all over to the house for us, and we've had dinner. The guys did a cookout and the food was amazing. All of it. Now, the little girls are being ushered out to the men with the rest of the kids so that I can open my bridal shower gifts. They decided to forgo the games this time because I am getting tired. Honestly, I don't care if we take the gifts home and I open them later. But, I can't do that to everyone here.

"Keegan, you just sit right where you are, and we'll bring everything over to you," Skylar tells me, as Rage is leaning in for a kiss.

"Are you sure you're up for this?" he asks me.

"No. But, they went through the trouble to do this for me, so I'm going to at least open the gifts. I'll let you know when I'm ready to head home."

"Don't be too long. I don't like the way you're lookin' firefly. You need to rest. I know you've been sittin' down, but it's not enough. We need to get you in bed with your feet up."

Rage is such a worry wart. I haven't had any issues with the pregnancy. I'm just tired quicker and I can't move around the way I used to be able to. On one hand, it drives me up a wall with how protective he is. But, it shows that he loves the twins and me and only wants the best for us. Kasey is picking up on it too and starting to watch me more and more every day.

"I love you! Go with the men and I'll see you soon."

"I love you firefly."

As soon as my man leaves the room, Darcy brings over her gift to me. Her face is scarlet, and I can't help but wonder what she got me. Opening the bag, I can already feel my face turning red as well. I pull out several toys in various shapes and sizes, extra batteries, and a nightie that is more string than anything.

"Oh wow! I don't know where to even begin! Thank you, Darcy," I say, putting the items back in the bag and setting it down beside me.

The girls are making comments over all the gifts I get. Honestly, I don't know who gave me the most outrageous one today. I've gotten everything from edible underwear to a sex swing to hang in the bedroom. There's a ton of new toys that we can have fun with. Even though I'm not usually one to include toys when I'm in the bedroom, I don't know that Rage will not want to try some of them out. I guess we'll just have to wait and see.

"Now, usually we'd include more games, but the bride to be is in need of rest. So, we're not going to do that tonight," Bailey tells everyone. "So, I've already messaged Rage and he'll be here in a minute to get you Keegan."

I nod my head, thankful that he's coming to get me. Hopefully we can take a truck over to the house because I'm exhausted. Normally, I'd walk, but I don't know that I can after today. It's been a long one and I'm ready to fall asleep where I sit right now.

Riley is standing by my side when Rage walks in the room to get me. Kasey is hot on his heels and I know she's going to ask me a hundred and one questions because I'm so tired. I love it though, and you'll never hear me complain. Surprisingly, she takes my hand while my man helps me up and then she takes Riley's hand. My friend has two plates loaded down with cake and other desserts in her hands for us to take home. Normally, I'm not one to pass up sweets, but I'm too tired to even look at the plates right now.

"Let's get you to bed firefly. Tomorrow, you're not doin' nothin'. Even if I have to have the girls come over and make sure you stay in bed!" Rage threatens as he leads me outside.

"I'm not going to argue that point at all babe. I don't want to move any more. I just want to go to sleep."

Rage chuckles, but I know that he's still going to make sure the girls are at the house tomorrow. They'll take care of everything I would normally do during the day. And I bet Skylar is already planning on what to make for dinner for us. She's good like that and we all love her cooking.

"I'm going to be over in the morning to watch Kasey," Sami announces, coming up to the passenger side of the truck. "Their vacation starts tomorrow, and she won't be in school. So, we'll spend the day together."

"Thank you so much Sami," I tell her, pulling her in for a hug. "If you want to come over tonight, you're more than welcome."

"No. Goose and I are going to the movies and a late dinner."

"Okay. Have fun and I'll see you in the morning."

We get to the house and Rage puts me to bed before making sure that Kasey does her nightly routine. This man is amazing and I'm so lucky to have him and his wonderful daughter in my life.

Chapter Twelve

Rage

A few weeks later

TONIGHT, I GUESS THE GUYS AND GIRLS are throwing Keegan and I parties before we get married. I can't believe that tomorrow the love of my life becomes mine in the eyes of the law. Kasey is excited and keeps telling us that she can't wait until Keegan is really her mama. What more could I ask for?

I'm not sure exactly what is planned for us tonight, but I'm sure that it's going to be crazy and we're going to end up getting in trouble. The same goes for the girls. I'm sure my girl is going to see, and hear, things she wished she didn't. Especially with Bailey planning the bachelorette party.

"You ready for tonight?" Grim asks, walking up and sitting at the bar with me.

"Yeah. I'm not sure what you guys have planned, but I hope Bailey takes it easy on my girl. Things have been rough with her the last week or so."

"What do you mean?" he asks, the concern evident on his face.

"I mean, she's tired all the time. She can barely move with how big she's gotten. And, her back hurts so bad. I spend more time rubbin' it for her than anythin' else. I'm not complainin', but I don't like seeing her in the pain she's in. It's to the point that she has a hard time sleepin' because she can't get comfortable."

"Isn't there anythin' they can do to help her?"

"I don't know. We go back to the doctor the day after the weddin'. Hell, I don't even know if we should go through with the weddin'."

"Why would you say that?" Bailey asks, her and Whitney walking up to us. "What's going on?"

"Nothin' like what you're thinkin' crazy girl," Grim answers her.

"Then why wouldn't you want to have the wedding?" Whitney asks.

"Keegan isn't feelin' all that great. You know how she's been feelin' and it's only gotten worse over the last few days."

"Fuck!" Bailey says. "Why doesn't she tell anyone? We'll help her out no questions asked."

"She knows that. Firefly doesn't want to feel like a burden to anyone though. Hell, it's like pullin' teeth just to get her to let me do anythin' to help her out."

"Okay. So, we'll change plans." Whitney responds.

"Don't tell her that you're doin' that either. It will upset her," I tell the girls, knowing that they won't say anything to her.

"We won't change much. Just the venue. You guys are going to be going to the strip club. So, we'll have it here instead. I'm sure you guys would feel safer with us here anyway."

"I know I would," Grim answers, taking a sip of his coffee.

Bailey gives a playful smack to Grim's arm before looking upset. We all know it's nothing more than an act, but it's funny. That's something I know I need right now. Whitney is trying to hide her laughter and failing miserably at it.

"I guess that just means that we get to have the prospects here to watch over us. They'll get to help us set up. And, they'll get to watch the male strippers I've hired," Bailey informs Grim.

"Crazy girl, you're tryin' to get me hurt, aren't you?" Grim asks, turning in his chair to look at his wife.

"Nope. Just know you're not going to leave us here alone."

"You have a point. Just try to be nice to them. I don't want to have to get more prospects because you've all scarred them for life."

"If they can't handle a few old ladies, do you really want them in the club?" she asks, making a valid point.

Grim shakes his head and I know that he's going to give in to her. It was never really a question though. Not when it comes to the comfort and safety of our women. I can already see my President relaxing knowing that they'll be here instead of some strip club. The girls tell us they're going to get everything they need to set up for tonight before walking out the door.

"I'm headin' home. Need to check on my girls," I tell Grim.

"Call if you need anythin'."

Walking in the door to the house, I can hear laughter coming from the bedroom. Kasey has been spending time with Keegan in bed. They play, watch movies, read, and paint one another's nails. Firefly is trying so hard to keep life and normal as possible for our little girl. Every day I fall more and more in love with her for that reason alone.

Standing in the doorway, I watch my daughter telling Keegan and Sami a story. She's being very animated, and her changing voices are over the top. No one notices me watching them until Kasey spins in a circle, almost falling, and I rush in to catch her.

"Daddy! You scared me," Kasey tells me, wrapping her little arms around my neck.

"I'm sorry sweet pea."

"Is okay. Did you hear my story?"

"I caught part of it. What are you talkin' about?" I ask her, sitting on the end of the bed.

"Jameson and Zoey. He gots mad because she didn't want to do what he wanted her to."

"Oh. Well, sometimes, he just wants to help protect you all."

"We know. It's just funny. He's like you and our uncas."

The three of us laugh at her description of Jameson. She's accurate in it. The boys have always been protective over the younger kids and it's only gotten worse as they've gotten older. Hell, in a year we're about to start having teenagers around here. Anthony will be the first one to hit his teens, but the rest of the kids aren't far behind him.

"How are you feelin' firefly?" I ask, putting my daughter down and walking over to get a kiss.

"I'm tired. But, that's nothing new these days. Sami is going to take Kasey to the clubhouse with some of the other kids to play so I can take a nap."

"Okay. I'm goin' to head over to check on a few of the buildin' sites. And, I think I have to go look at a few houses that are goin' up for auction. We're thinkin' of buyin' them for more shelter homes."

"That's amazing!" Keegan tells me on a yawn.

Kissing my girl again, I head out to go to work for a little bit. She needs uninterrupted sleep time if she's finally comfortable enough to finally get some sleep. Sami and Kasey walk out with me and we all head out. Pulling out my phone, I call over to the clubhouse to send a prospect over to keep an eye on my girl. I don't want her to be alone if anything happens.

Today has been long and I'm glad it's finally over. Going to the job sites wasn't that bad. I checked in, order materials for the guys to pick up, and made sure the foremen had everything under control. I'll be back full time once the twins are born, but right now, I need to be there for Keegan. My employees understand this and always ask how things are going.

It wasn't too bad looking at the first four houses that are going up for auction. Unfortunately, the same can't be said for the last two. They are in dire need of repair and I don't know if Grim and the guys are going to want to put the money in to them. It's a shame though because they're both in ideal locations. They're by the clubhouse, but on a lot of land. The houses sit back so you have to know they're there to find them. These would be the houses to use for children with disabilities. I know the girls have been reading up on different therapies for disabled children including the use of animals. I'll bring that point up when I talk to them about the places and see what happens.

Pulling up to the house, I see a few cars and Skylar, Cage, and Joker walking up to the porch.

Immediately my mind goes to something being wrong. So, I jump out of the truck after barely taking the time to put it in park and shut it off. Running to the door, I see the guys stopping and waiting for me to get there. Skylar is already inside and that's where I want to be. That's where I *need* to be.

"Where's the fire Rage?" Joker asks.

"What's wrong with Keegan?" I ask, worry and concern lacing my voice.

"Nothin'. The girls are over here helpin' her get ready to go tonight."

"Thank God!" I breath out, trying to calm myself down.

"Fuck! You seriously thought somethin' was wrong?" Cage asks.

"Yeah. I saw the cars and you guys and immediately went into panic mode. I know how firefly has been feelin' and it's not good."

"Sorry man. You know we would've called you though."

"I know. I just can't help but worry about her and the twins."

"We've been there. We know what you're goin' through. Go see your girl, get a shower, and get ready. We're leavin' in a half hour." Cage responds, walking into the house.

Even though I know my girl is okay, I still practically run to the bedroom to see her. I need to lay eyes on her. Opening the door, I see her sitting on the edge of the bed. She's wearing a black dress that shows off our babies and leaves her upper back and arms bare. Keegan looks amazing. Turning her eyes to me, I see the pure happiness radiating from her.

"Hey babe!" she greets me. "You okay?"

"I am now. You look gorgeous firefly," I tell her, walking over for a kiss.

Darcy, who is working on her hair, backs away so I can get some lovin' from my girl. Keegan wraps her arms around me and pours everything she has into this kiss. Honestly, I want nothing more than to kick everyone out and show her how much I love her and how happy I am to see a smile gracing her face again. That can't happen right now though.

"Later," I murmur in her ear.

"Promise?" she asks breathlessly.

"Absolutely. Don't get too tired firefly."

She nods her head as I grab some clothes and make my way into the bathroom. Quickly showering, I am ready to go in record time. The quicker we leave, the quicker I can get back home. That's the only thought on my mind as I walk back in the bedroom and see Keegan sitting on the bed alone.

Darcy has curled her hair and left is flowing down her back. Whoever did her make-up made her look like she's not wearing any at all. The glow radiating from her outdoes all that though. Looking at my girl, I fall in love all over again. She's so pure and light I can't help but want to be surrounded by her.

I give her a lingering kiss that neither one of us want to stop. Unfortunately, we both have to go. Everyone in the club is waiting on us. While it is our night, they have gone through planning a special night for us, so we can't stay home. This is our family pulling together to show us how much we mean to one another. And, I'm pretty sure that we're going to Dander Falls so that the girls could stay here. Not that I want to be that far away from Keegan right now.

"We have to go," I say, finally pulling away from my girl.

"I know. Have fun tonight and I'll see you later."

"What do you mean you'll see him later?" Skylar asks, coming to the door.

"When the parties are over, we're comin' back home." I answer like it's the most logical thing in the world to expect.

"No. You can come home. You're not seeing her until she walks down the aisle tomorrow," she informs us.

"What the fuck?" I bellow out. "Why is that?"

"It's tradition. You can't see the bride the night before the wedding."

"I am goin' to be seein' my girl. No one can stop me!"

"Not happening stud. You can wait until tomorrow. It's late morning so you won't have long to wait."

I can tell by the tone of her voice and her stance that Skylar is going to stick to this rule. And I was planning on coming home to show Keegan just what she means to me. She's finally feeling good enough to do something, not that I'm complaining about the lack of sex. I want to take full advantage, so I hope tomorrow she feels just as good as tonight.

"Alright babe, have fun and I'll see you in the morning," Keegan tells me, leaning in for another kiss.

"Firefly, be safe and if you need me, call. I don't want to hear any nonsense about you not wantin' to interrupt my night. I'll call and text throughout the night."

"Okay. I love you!"

"Love you too firefly," I tell her, giving her one more scorching kiss before walking out the door.

We arrived at the Kitty Kat Lounge and see that Gage has closed the club for the night. This amazes me because I know it's one of their busier nights, Friday. I never expected them to do this. I figured he'd set something up so that the guys from all three clubs could party and be separate from the rest of the strip club.

"Gage, why did you close the club?" I ask.

"We're havin' a party for you and I don't want any interruptions. It's not a big deal," he responds with a shrug of his shoulders.

"It is to me. Thank you, brother!"

I'm pulled by Grim to one of the tables in the front by the stage. Crash, Trojan, Killer, and Slim are already sitting there. They all give me head nods before turning back to the stage to watch the show already going on. I'm not sure who the girl on stage is, but she doesn't hold a candle to Keegan. I still appreciate a beautiful woman, but the girl up there now, looks young. That's not my thing.

"What are the girls gettin' up to tonight?" Slim asks Grim, who has taken the seat next to me and handed me a drink.

"Bailey hired some strippers. Other than that, it's goin' to be pretty chill. They don't want Keegan to overdo it."

"She hired what?" Crash and Trojan ask at the same time.

"Don't get your fuckin' panties in a twist. Darcy hasn't ever seen strippers before. She's not goin' to know what to do so she'll probably sit back with Keegan and just enjoy the show. Same thing you two are doin' right now," Grim responds.

"I don't fuckin' think so!" Crash bellows, standing up.

"Sit the fuck down!" Gage says. "You want this girl to be yours then let her have her fuckin' fun! You two go in there all cavemen and ruin tonight for them and she really won't talk to you. You'll never find out what's goin' on with her."

Crash reluctantly sit's back down, knowing that his President is right. Darcy is slowly coming around to the idea of them wanting her. Even if she's not admitting it to herself. Anyone that sees the three of them together can see the longing and lust in her eyes. I can see the two men looking around the strip club and I know who they're looking for. Wood.

"Where the fuck is he?" Trojan asks Slim.

"Who?" Slim asks, innocently.

"Wood."

"Oh, he's on babysittin' duty with Boy Scout. I think they're almost to Clifton Falls."

This time Trojan stands up so fast his chair flies backwards and crashes into the table next to us. Slim is trying to hide the smile playing on his lips. Out of the corner of my eye I see Wood coming from the back, fixing his pants. Now, I can't help the laughter from escaping.

"The fuck you laughin' at?" Trojan asks me. "He's the one that gave your girl her nickname. And they went crashin' to the floor when we were all shoppin'."

"You're right. But, I know my girl has eyes only for me. I'm not goin' to let a few accidents bend my dick out of shape."

"What's up guys?" Wood asks, walking up to the table.

Trojan and Crash look from Wood to Slim and I can see the rage building. Slim starts laughing so hard I wonder how he'll stay upright in his chair. Especially holding his beer. The rest of us can't contain our laughter anymore. Meanwhile, Wood is standing there trying to figure out what's going on.

"That will teach you not to trust a brother and your woman," Slim tells them when he finally catches his breath.

The two men sit down and look at their drinks. They know that they're in the wrong, but when it comes to Darcy they can't help it. If Keegan was being standoffish like she is, I'd probably be the same way. Something has spooked her and she's afraid to give them a chance at being something great. Add in everything that has happened between her and Wood, and I'd be worse than these two have been.

Wood joins us just as one of the strippers comes up and starts rubbing herself all over me. I could honestly care less about her fake tit's and over made up face. She thinks she got it, and for some she may. I don't like the look though.

"I hear tonight is your last night as a single man, baby," she purrs in my ear. "Why don't you let me show you a good time?"

"Nope. Just because I'm not married yet, doesn't mean I'll cheat on my girl. She means more to me than a few minutes with you."

"No one has to know baby," she continues to try, running her hand down my chest towards my cock.

"Not. Happening," I tell her again, grabbing her hand and pulling it off my body.

"Harley, get ready to go on stage or leave for the night. He's not here for pussy, he's here for a good night," Gage says, coming over to the table.

"Yes, Gage. I'm sorry," she says, walking to the back of the building.

"Sorry Rage. She's been tryin' to get someone's attention for the last month. I'm not sure what's goin' on with her, but she won't open up. Can't help if I don't know what's goin' on."

"It's all good Gage. None of your guys like her?"

"There's one that does. I'm just not sure he'll go for it. She's a good girl, talks a big game. I doubt she would've done anythin' with you if you went in a room with her. I've heard from a few guys that she'd rather talk to them or give them a massage. Somethin' simple like that," Gage responds, taking a sip of his beer.

Pulling out my phone, I send a message to Keegan. I need to check in with her. For some reason, I'm getting a weird feeling and I don't know why. The threat from Sam and her dad is gone, so I don't know what else could go wrong.

Me: Everythin' good firefly?

I take a sip of my drink while I wait for a response. It's been a few minutes and I'm ready to send another message or call when my phone beeps.

Keegan: I'm good. Having fun with the girls. You should see Darcy.

Before I can ask what she means, another message comes through. It's a picture of Darcy on a table dancing. She's surrounded by the strippers and I can make out one of the prospects trying to get to her. Holy fuck! Trojan and Crash will go ballistic if they see this. Grim, Gage, and Slim all start laughing their asses off when I show them the picture. Thankfully the other two aren't paying any attention to what we're doing. Looks like the girls are having a good time.

Me: Love you firefly. Can't wait to see you tomorrow mornin'.

Keegan: Love you more!

Keegan

Sitting in the clubhouse, I'm drinking virgin drinks while the rest of the girls are getting drunk. I'm having a good time watching them all let loose. Especially Darcy and Riley. Those two really need it. Maddie sits down next to me, and I admire the work Riley did on her hair again. Riley is an excellent hair stylist and I can't wait to get her to do my hair again.

About an hour after we got here, the strippers Bailey hired showed up. I could see the looks exchanged by the prospects. I'm sure they'd rather be anywhere else but here right now. But, I guess they're on babysitting duty tonight. They've been keeping my glass full and making sure that I don't need anything else. Hell, one of them even brought me over a plate of food right before the strippers got here.

"Are you having fun?" Maddie slurs out.

"I am. I'm almost grateful that I can't drink tonight seeing how quick you all got drunk."

"Bailey makes some potent shit," she answers.

Her mouth drops open when the strippers start putting on a show for us. I can just imagine the thoughts running through her head right now. But, I'm sure the only man starring in those thoughts is Tank. He's gorgeous and I know they love one another the way I love Rage.

Before too long, all the girls are sitting in a semi-circle enjoying the show. I'm not sure exactly what got into Darcy, other than strong drinks, but she ends up on a table dancing. I start snapping a few pictures. The male dancers suddenly surround her, and I can see the prospects getting nervous. Everyone knows that Crash and Trojan won't be happy if anything happens to Darcy, or someone puts their hands on her. Especially when it comes to other men. We better get her down from there.

Just as I go to try to stand, I get a message on my phone. It takes me a minute to pull it out because somehow it fell between the side of the chair and my leg. I'm trying to pull it out when Riley comes to my aid. She grabs the phone and hands it to me. She's had a few drinks, but is definitely the soberest one here that can drink.

"Thank you! It would've taken me forever to get it out."

"It's okay. I'm going to go see if I can help Darcy out."

I see that it's a message from Rage and I feel the smile break out on my face. To show him some of the shit the girls have been up to, I send him one of the pictures of Darcy on the table. It's kind of funny and I hope that he doesn't show her men. Guess we'll find out if they come storming in here.

Looking up after telling my man I love him, I see that not only are the strippers down to their little underwear, if you can call it that. But some of the girls are also beginning to lose their clothes. Oh my! Darcy is on the table, Bailey is down to her leggings and bra, Skylar is in the process of stripping out of her shirt, and Maddie and Melody are sitting on the sidelines looking like they want to join the party and strip. I don't know why they just don't go for it.

"The prospects are the only ones here, go for it. I can see that you want to," I tell them.

Maddie and Melody look at me and after shrugging their shoulders, the two stand up and join the rest of the girls. I laugh at their antics until I know I have to go to the bathroom. One of the prospects sees my dilemma and runs over to help me get up. Just as I go to stand up though, I feel a sharp pain in my back. It almost takes me to my knees and the prospects looks at me while pulling his phone out.

"Don't you dare make that call!" I tell him, breathing through the pain. "I'm going to interrupt his night for no reason."

"But,"

"There is no 'but.' I'm fine. See, it's already starting to go away. I haven't had any other pain. It's probably just from me sitting in the same position for so long," I tell him, standing all the way up again. "Thank you for helping me. I'll be fine now."

Making my way to the bathroom, I'm waddling as fast as I can. Hopefully I make it in time and don't have to go back over to the house to change my clothes. That would really suck! But, it's one of the joys of being pregnant I guess.

As soon as I walk back in to the main room, the strippers are descending on me. Oh lord! What have the girls done while I was gone for a whole five minutes? They lead me over to a chair that has been moved to the middle of the floor and help me sit down. Before I can say or do anything, they're all dancing around me. It's like getting multiple lap dances at one time. Don't get me wrong, all the men are hot as hades, but there's no way they'll ever compare to Rage.

Not knowing what to do, I just sit there and let them do their thing. Bailey walks over to me and brings my hands up to rub down one guy's chest. This is not happening right now! I can only imagine what Rage will think if he catches wind of this. So, I pull my hands back and cover my face as a barely covered cock is right there.

"Come on Keegan, get a few touches in before you're a married woman!" Skylar calls out to me. And to think I thought she was the mild one.

"I'm good. Thanks though," I say, my face turning a bright red.

No matter where I look right now, there's a cock in my face. What am I supposed to do now? Darcy is down off the table and making her way over to us though. I'll pull her in and let her have some fun. It's what friends do, right?

Darcy is in all her glory as Riley helps me out of the chair and away from the dancing, almost naked men. Man, I wish I could have a drink right now! It would make dealing with a bunch of drunk girls easier. Hell, I would be having as much fun as they are right now. I'm having fun, just not quite as much as them. I'll be the one to tell them all about it though. I guarantee none of them will remember tonight though.

It's been a few more hours of dancing men and drinking girls. I've been given food, water, and virgin drinks all night long. At some point, one of the girls put a tiara on my head and a sash around me. I'm ready to fall asleep now, and I know some of the girls are starting to pass out.

The same prospect from earlier comes over to help me out of the chair and I make my way into the room I share with Rage and Kasey when we're here. Just as I'm getting out of the dress so I can get in bed, my phone rings. I smile when I see the picture of Rage and me from getting our pregnancy photos done.

"Hey baby," I answer the phone.

"Hey firefly. It's quiet there," he responds.

"I'm in our room. The girls are slowly starting to pass out and I'm beyond exhausted."

"Why didn't you go back to the room sooner then?" he asks, the concern lacing his voice.

"I was having fun. And I wasn't doing anything more than sitting in a chair. The prospects waited on me hand and foot. They helped me when I needed to get out of the chair and everything."

"Yeah, and what's with the pain you felt a few times that took your breath away and almost dropped you to your knees?" he asks.

"I told him not to interrupt your night. It's not a big deal baby. I'm fine, the babies are fine, and we'll see what the doctor has to say in less than two days."

"I still don't like it firefly," he says. "I'd rather be there with you in case you need me. What if somethin' happens and I'm still an hour and a half away."

"You'll do what you need to in order to get here as fast and as safe as you can," I answer him, laying down in bed and trying to get comfortable.

"You layin' down firefly?" he asks, and I can hear him shuffling around.

"Yeah. Are you?"

"I am. I'm missin' havin' you in my arms firefly."

"I'm missing you too. I can't wait until I get to see you tomorrow."

"It won't get here soon enough. I'll let you go so you can get to sleep firefly. I love you more than you know."

"I love you to the moon and back."

Laying down, I rearrange the pillows and blankets until I can get comfortable. Falling into a deep sleep, I let myself go because I know it's not going to last long. Between being uncomfortable and having to pee, I'll be up every so often.

Chapter Thirteen

Keegan

WAKING UP THIS MORNING, I'm more than ready to marry the love of my life. However, my most important concern right now is having to relieve my bladder. The bed is low enough that I can do this rolling out of bed maneuver to get out of it.

As soon as I'm done on the toilet, I jump in the shower. I know that the girls are going to be in here any minute now to help me start getting ready. Since I'm showering alone, I get everything done as quickly as I can. It's kind of hard to do certain things so Rage will have to help me out later on.

Yesterday and today I have felt really good. I'm still tired and my back is still killing me. But, I want to do more around the house and I want to make sure everything is truly ready for when the twins get here. Whitney and Melody both told me that I'm nesting. They say that I'm going to be giving birth soon. I can only hope so at this point.

Once I'm back in the room, I hear pounding on the door. It's too soft to be Rage or any of the guys so I'm going to guess that the girls are here and anxious to get things moving along. Probably Rage got back and is running his mouth to get things going. I can totally see him going all caveman because he wants to see me. I guess it's a good thing that one of the brothers are performing the ceremony for us, so we can really start it whenever we want to.

A big part of me can't wait to see my man. But, another part of me can't wait to see what the girls have done as far as decorations. I gave colors I liked and a general idea. The girls took charge and wouldn't let Rage, or I help out with anything else. It was to the point that I'm surprised I got to pick out what dress I wanted to wear. Thankfully, I love these girls and I'm glad they took charge so it was one less thing I was concentrating on while pregnant.

"Ready to get beautiful?" Sami asks, leading the way in the room.

"I am. I've already showered and now I'm ready to get dressed and whatever else you guys want to do to me."

"Good. Rage is going crazy out there. He wants to lay eyes on you now. I'm pretty sure all the guys, including the kids, are ready to go already. We're just waiting on you," Bailey tells me.

Looking at them, I see that all the girls are ready. The only ones missing are the little girls. I'm trying to peer around everyone to see them in their little dresses. They're not there though.

"Alice took them out to get pictures started," Skylar tells us.

"Alright, lets get going then. I don't want to keep Rage waiting. I want to see him just as bad as he wants to see me."

The girls all surround me and help me get dressed and my hair done. Once again, Darcy curled my hair. Instead of leaving it down though, she pulled the sides back leaving just a few tendrils down around my face. Melody is the one to do my make-up today and it's understated. Honestly, it doesn't even look like I'm wearing any. The only thing giving it away is the light color on my eyelids and the sweep of tinted lip gloss on my lips.

"You look absolutely stunning!" Maddie gushes. "Let's get you out for a few pictures so we can get you to your man."

Bailey makes a phone call to make sure that Rage isn't going to see me before we leave the room. I'm guessing that she called Pops since he meets us in the hallway. He's dressed in a nice-looking pair of jean, a long sleeve dress shirt, and his cut.

"I know things have been crazy Keegan. And I know that you have Kasey, but I'd be honored if I could walk you down the aisle to Rage," Pops tells me.

"I'd be honored," I tell him, the tears flowing down my face.

He holds out his arm for me and I put my hand in the crutch of his arm. We walk out to the photographer telling us how she wants us to stand and pose. The final picture she takes before the wedding is Kasey standing in front of me, facing me with her little hands on each side of my belly. She's kind of leaning in like she's going to give the babies a kiss. It's going to be one of the cutest pictures and I can't wait to see the proofs. This one is definitely going on the wall.

"Alright, Rage is having a fit," Bailey tells us.

"I'm ready. I need to see my man," I tell them.

Alice leads the kids to the back door so that we can all line up and head outside. The prospects are guarding the door so that no one can see in before I step a foot outside. Everyone is really making sure that Rage has to wait to see me. I can't wait to see him and I'm about ready to just push past everyone so that I can see my man. It's been too long, and we were only apart since yesterday afternoon.

Finally, it's my turn to walk down the aisle and I gasp as soon as I step foot outside. Everything is done in reds and crèmes. I didn't want traditional white. There's flowers along the aisle where the bikes aren't parked and crème colored ribbon cascading down the backs of chairs. The runner we're walking up is crème colored outlined in red with red double hearts. My heart is melting at the attention to detail these girls have put into our wedding.

Rage is standing at the front looking as handsome as I've ever seen him. He's wearing a dark red long-sleeved dress shirt with his cut over it and a dark pair of new jeans. I want nothing more than to run to him right now. But, being as pregnant as I am, that wouldn't work out to well. I'd probably look like a whale trying to get to her food. Or I'd trip and fall all over myself. So, I let Pops lead me to him at his pace. He speeds up a little bit and I see the smirk gracing his face.

I'm finally standing next to my man in front of Slim. I knew that one of the guys were doing the ceremony, I just didn't know it was going to be him. Honestly, I'm glad that it's him. I grew to look up to him when I stayed in Benton Falls. I'm honored that he's performing the ceremony and Pops wanted to walk me down the aisle.

"Who gives this woman to this man?" he asks.

"I do along with the rest of the Wild Kings and Phantom Bastards members," Pops responds before placing a kiss on my cheek and putting my hand in Rage's.

The rest of the ceremony seems to go by in a blur as I stare in Rage's eyes. Finally, we're to the part where we exchange vows. The only thing that we have control over was the vows we chose to write for one another. I know I've spent a lot of time on mine so that I could make sure that everything I wanted to say to Rage and Kasey was included.

"Keegan, my world has been ripped apart more times than I can count. Now, when it's turnin' upside down, I look at you and instantly I feel calm. You have given me so much from the love you show our little girl to the love you show me and the twins that you're carryin' now. I'll never be able to tell you how much I love you, but I will show you every day for the rest of our lives. You will be cherished and loved from now until forever."

"Rage, I have spent my entire life running and hiding from a monster, one that you helped slay. My life became complete with one look from you and one word from our beautiful little sweet pea. The twins that we're waiting on now are going to do nothing but add to our joy and love. I'll never be able to show you the love I feel for both of you, but I'll try my hardest every single day for the rest of our lives and beyond."

After exchanging rings, Slim pronounces us husband and wife and tells us to kiss. As Rage lays a scorching kiss on me, I can hear the revving of the bike's engines and know that today is perfect. We're surrounded by our family and there's nothing that can ruin today. Kasey wrapping her arms around both of our legs is the only thing that stops us from putting on a show right here for everyone. Looking down, I see tears running down her little face and Rage bends down to pick her up.

"What's the matter sweet pea?" he asks.

"Nothing. My heart is happy, and these are happy tears," she tells us.

I can feel the tears gathering and I look up to see tears in my man's eyes too. This little girl can slay us with just a few words and we don't care who sees it. The ones that are surrounding us heard what she said, and I hear a few sniffles from them.

"Let's get inside," Rage says. "I need a few minutes with my girls."

"No, you needs a few minutes with mama. I want to see Zoey," Kasey tells us.

We both start laughing at the fact that Kasey now wants nothing to do with us, but wants to be with her little friends. Bailey reminds us that we still have to get pictures done before we head inside for a second. Rage leads me to our room and take a few seconds just to hold me and check me over. I knew it was just a matter of time before he gave me a complete once over after hearing that I've been having pains in my back.

"How are you feelin' today, wife?" he asks me.

"I'm good. Today is perfect and I want to enjoy it for a little bit with our family," I tell him. I know if we stay in this room for much longer, we won't be coming back out the rest of the night.

"Alright. Let's get these pictures done so we can go to this reception for a little while. Alice and Pops are takin' Kasey for the night and I'm ready to have you all to myself."

"Sounds like a plan to me."

Rage

Finally, Keegan is my wife and my old lady. She's got my rag on after the ceremony for our pictures and my rings on her finger. The only thing that would make today better is if the next two members of our family were here with us. But, it's not going to be long now.

It seems like we were posed for pictures forever. But, it's over with now and I lead my wife over to our table. After sitting her down, I get the three of us some food so that my babies are all fed. Kasey joins us to eat before running off again to play with the rest of the kids. We're not alone though. Someone is always coming over to congratulate us or ask Keegan how she's feeling. One of the prospects is even hovering to make sure that I don't have to leave her side for any length of time.

"Are you ready to dance?" I ask my girl.

"Yeah. One dance is all I can manage though," she tells me.

I'm getting tired and today has taken it's toll on me. It doesn't matter that I haven't really had to do anything, everything takes a toll on me. Rage leads me out to the make-shift dance floor as one of the prospects announces our dance. He wanted to be the one to pick our song, so I wait in anticipation to hear what he's chosen. *Making My Way To You* by *Cole Swindell* comes on and I start chuckling. One night in bed we talked about this song and he told me that if we ever got married this was going to be our song. I should've remembered that.

"What's funny?" he asks, looking down into my eyes.

"I was just remembering the conversation we had about this song."

"I told you what our song was goin' to be."

I lay my head on his chest and we continue to gently move and sway to the music. Before the song is over, I get another sharp pain in my back without any warning. Rage barely holds me up I drop so fast. This one is definitely worse than anything I felt yesterday.

"Firefly!" he yells. "What's the matter?"

"Pain," I pant out, looking down and seeing a giant wet spot on the front of my dress.

Rage follows my line of sight and I can feel him tense up. He knows that these babies are going to making their appearance today. I'm not scared or nervous. Instead I feel a joy like no other. It seems that the rest of our little family has decided that they want to be a part of our special day after all.

Chapter Fourteen

Rage

I'VE NEVER SEEN ANYONE IN AS much pain as what I'm watching my wife go through right now. As soon as we realized that her water broke, a few of the guys brought over anything they could find to lay her down on. I'm not sure if that's what we were supposed to do, but she seemed to be in a little less pain right now then when she was standing up or bending over.

We've been at the hospital for a few hours and Keegan is doing amazing. She's trying not to take anything for the pain, but I can see the pain is taking it's toll on her body and she wants some relief. I'm not going to say a single word if she decides that she needs to take something to help her out.

"Rage, I think we need to rethink this whole medicine thing," she finally tells me.

"It's up to you firefly. If you want to have somethin' you get it. I stand by any decision you make," I tell her, wiping her forehead with the wet cloth again.

"Can you push the button to get a nurse in here please?" she asks as another contraction hit's her.

I do as she asks and help her know where she is in her contraction. That seems to help her somehow and I'm going to do anything that I can to help her through this process. We're going to get through this together, even when she's yelling at me, telling me she hates me, that she's going to cut my dick off, everything. At the end of the day, I know that she doesn't mean any of it and we're going to be so happy and fall in love when we see our babies.

"What can I do for you?" a nurse asks, walking in the room and checking the monitors.

"I need something for the pain please," Keegan tells her. "I'm not going to last any longer without something."

"Let me check you and we'll see what we can do," she responds.

While I don't really want to watch some female stick her finger in my wife, I know that it's a part of the process. My concern is making sure that my wife and the twins are okay, and we do what we have to do to protect all three of them. After checking Keegan, the nurse tells us that she's going to have to talk to the doctor before she will be able to do anything.

"What's goin' on?" I ask immediately, wanting to know why she can't just give her something now.

"She's too close to not being able to give her anything. So, I want to see what Doctor Sanchez wants to do."

"Please?" Keegan begs. "I can't do this anymore. I'm so tired and I'm not going to be able to push these babies out."

"I'll make sure that she knows. You've been doing so good and we'll do what is best for everyone involved honey," the nurse says before leaving the room.

Honestly, I think I scare her a little bit. But, I don't really care. Not when it comes to the safety of my family. And this instance is literally a matter of life and death in my eyes. One wrong move could injure my unborn children. I'm not going to have it.

"It will be okay firefly," I tell her, trying to make sure that she remains as calm as she can right now.

Before too long, Doctor Sanchez comes in and checks my wife herself. She agrees with the nurse and tells us that we don't have many options right now. Her main concern is the safety of the twins. So, she tells Keegan that we may have to think about going the route of a cesarean section. Right after she says that, she checks the papers printing out from the monitor. I'm not sure what she's looking for, but I'm going to go with whatever she says. Hopefully Keegan is on the same page.

"What do you think is going to be the best option?" my girl asks.

"At this point, I think we may want to prep you for the surgery," she answers honestly. "If you weren't so tired, I probably wouldn't be saying that. Rage has talked to me about the lack of sleep you've been getting though. The final decision is yours though."

Keegan looks at me and I can see that she's already made her mind up. "I want to have it done. Knowing my own body, I know that I'm not going to last much longer. I don't want to take any chances with our babies."

"I'll let everyone know," the doctor tells us before making her way out of the room.

"Why don't you go let everyone know what's going on?" Keegan asks me.

"I don't want to leave you. I'll send Grim a message and he can let everyone know," I tell her, pulling my phone out.

Keegan nods her head and closes her eyes. She's been trying to rest the best she can in between contractions. They've been getting closer together though, so it's not really working anymore. Hell, before I can even finish typing the message out, another one hit's her.

I continue to let her know where the contraction is until it's finally over with. Then I finish the message before putting my phone away again. About the same time, a nurse comes in to let us know that I have to leave her side to get gowned up. This is not going to work for me. Since Skylar has been through this before, she's knocking on the door.

"I don't mean to interrupt your time together, I just know that Rage isn't going to want to leave you alone," she tells us. "Would it be okay if I sit with her while you get ready?"

"Are you sure?" I ask her.

"Yeah. I've been through this a time or two," she says a smile gracing her face.

"Is that okay with you firefly?"

"Yeah. Get ready so we can meet our son and daughter."

I give her a kiss and follow the nurse out of the room. Really, I don't want to be getting ready while she's in another room, but it's going to take the least amount of time so I'm doing it. Skylar will know what Keegan needs while I'm not in there. I just hope that it doesn't take too long to bring her in the operating room our babies will be delivered in.

Keegan

I know that Rage didn't want to leave me alone, but he did it because he'll always do what is needed for the safety of his loved ones. There's no one he loves more than his children and then me. Skylar has been amazing in his absence though. She knows exactly what I need without me saying a word.

"Are you ready to go?" Doctor Sanchez asks.

"I'm more than ready," I tell her honestly.

The nurses that came in the room with her are busy getting everything ready for me to go. Skylar stays by my side through the entire process. Finally, they're ready to wheel me to the operating room. She walks with me as far as she can before making her way back to the rest of our family.

Rage is waiting for me and makes his way to my side as soon as he's allowed to. He takes a seat on the stool by my head as they make the final preparations. He's holding my hand and telling me how proud of me he is.

"Keegan and Rage, I'm about to make the incision that's needed to deliver the twins. Once I get it made, it's not going to be long before they'll be out. Here we go."

I don't feel a thing as Doctor Sanchez does what she has to do. Before too long, I do feel a little bit of pressure though. Right after that, we hear the cries of our first baby.

"It's a girl!" Doctor Sanchez announces.

With the curtain they have up, I can't see a thing so I ask Rage to stand up so he can see our baby. He does as I ask, not that I could really stop him if that's what he wanted to do. I can feel his body trembling and I know it's from the anticipation of seeing our daughter and having our son born next.

"It's a boy!" she announces second.

Tears are streaming down my face as our son and daughter are finally here. I can't wait to lay my eyes on them and see their perfect little faces. Rage is standing by my side watching all of the activity like a hawk. He's trying to keep his eyes on both babies at one time.

Finally, they bring our daughter over to us and hand her over to her daddy. He's immediately head over heels in love with her, it's written all over his face. Next a nurse brings our son over and hands him to Rage. I've never seen a better sight in my life. We're just missin one extremely important person to make this picture complete.

I'm back in my room and trying to rest. I don't want to close my eyes and miss a second with the babies though. Rage, seeing my dilemma, tells me that if I don't try to get some rest he'll have the babies taken to the nursery. I know he doesn't want them out of our sight. So, I lay back a little more and close my eyes.

I'm not sure how much time has passed, but I wake up to crying. Instantly I look around for my twins. Their daddy is changing one of them so that he can bring them over to be fed. Before he's done changing one baby, the other one starts crying. So, I try to get out of bed to help him.

"Don't even think about it," he tells me without taking his attention off the baby in front of him. "I'm almost done so you can feed him."

I sit back and take down the front of my gown so that I can nurse our son while he tends to his little princess. Kasey needs to be in here with us. As soon as I'm done feeding them, I'm going to tell Rage we need her in here with us. Everyone else can wait a few minutes, but we need our daughter with us right now.

Our son eats, and I hand him back over to his daddy while he hands me our daughter. Just from looking at them now, I think we both got our wish. Rage wanted a daughter that looked like me and I wanted our son to look like him. They each look like both of us, but she looks like me and he looks like his daddy. The best of both worlds if you ask me.

"Can you bring in Kasey please? I want a few minutes with just us before everyone else descends on us."

"I was thinkin' the same thing."

Rage leaves and is back before I know it with our daughter in his arms. He takes her to the first bassinet and leans her over so she can see her baby sister. Kasey tells us how pretty she is before leaning over to see her brother.

"Daddy, he looks just likes you," she tells us. "And sissy looks just likes mama!"

"You're right," Rage tells her, laughter in his voice.

"Takes me to mama please?" she asks.

He brings her over to me and carefully sets her down on the bed beside me. She leans on my shoulder and wraps one little arm around the back of my neck. I wrap my arms around her and hold her close. If there was any way for her to have been in here with us, I would've had her with us. I just don't think she was ready for this though.

While we're spending some family time together, she tells us all about what she did while waiting to come in here with us. We're both laughing at the description of the men pacing back and forth and talking about 'grown-up stuff.' Then she tells us that Alice brought lots of games, books, and puzzles for the kids to keep them occupied. I'm surprised they didn't stay at the clubhouse, but they're family so I'm glad that everyone is here.

"What are their names mama?" Kasey suddenly asks me.

"Well, your little sister's name is Lyric Rayne. And your brother's name is Tyler Jaxon."

"I likes those names," she tells us. "Do I gets to tell everyone?"

"Do you want to?" Rage asks her.

"Please?" she begs, giving her dad those puppy dog eyes neither one of can ever turn down.

"Yes. Let me go get them."

Kasey and I sit together and wait for everyone to get in the room. It doesn't take long, especially for the women. They're so impatient to see the newest additions to the family. Bailey is carrying boxes with her and I can bet I know what's inside them. I've heard all about her taking over the giving of the outfits from her mom.

Once everyone is in the room, Kasey wait's until she has everyone's attention before letting them know the names of the babies. "My new baby's names are Lyrics Rayne and Tylers Jaxon."

The women all 'ooh' and 'ahh' over the names while the men all offer congratulations to their brother. Everyone is gathering around the bassinets and I know that it's killing Rage to have them so close to Tyler and Lyric. He's doing a great job of hiding his reaction though. I'm so proud of him. I can only imagine how he's going to be once we get home with all the kids.

Epilogue One

Keegan

One year later

THE LAST YEAR HAS BEEN AMAZING. It took us a little bit to get into a routine, but once we found one that worked for us, there was no stopping us. Rage has been the overprotective dad I knew he was going to be. There's been a few times that I told him to go out with the guys or I was going to go out with the girls with all the kids. He left for a while so that he wasn't hovering. I didn't necessarily want him to leave, but he needed to get out with some grown-ups.

I love that he wants to spend time with his children to see them learn and grow every day, but we both need to get out of the house too. That's been another challenge to overcome. Rage trusts everyone in the club with his life, but he's hesitant to leaving Lyric and Tyler with anyone. He'd rather be there for everything than have help. I've helped him see that we need time away with our friends and time away together.

Today is the twin's birthday. Rage is out getting the last-minute things we need while I help the girls decorate the pond. Jameson and Anthony are helping us keep and eye on the kids while we get everything set up. Grim and Tank are with us making sure the grill is ready to go so they can start cooking soon.

"Dada! Dada!" I hear Tyler call out.

Looking up from blowing up the kids floaties, I fall more in love with my husband. He's carrying the cakes we ordered over to the tables while paying attention to Tyler. He's been followed by the twins as they're curious about every little thing around them. Once he sets the cakes down, he lifts them both up in his arms and lets them see their cake. Lyric starts clapping her hands and laughing. Tyler is trying to get closer to his cake almost throwing his dad off balance. He's definitely got Rage's stubborn streak.

Rage and our children find ways every day to make me love them more and drive me crazy all at the same time. I wouldn't change my life in any way though. I have a wonderful and crazy family, including the extended family members, I get closer to the girls every day, and Sami and Whitney are becoming as close to me as cousins should be. My life turned out better than I ever dreamed possible.

Rage

I wouldn't change the last year for anything in the world. It's been crazy and hectic at times, Keegan has kicked me out of the house once or twice, and Kasey is teaching her brother and sister everything she knows. I'm in trouble for sure. Especially when all three of them gang up on me and pull out the pouty lips and puppy dog eyes. I can't tell them no.

After eating lunch, Tyler and Lyric couldn't wait any longer to get their cake. We stripped them down and, after singing 'Happy Birthday' to them, we let them have at it. I've never seen such little faces covered in so much icing and cake. Both of them basically smashed their face directly into their piece of cake before picking up the parts that weren't already stuck to their faces with their little fists. I have a ton of pictures of them and I know Keegan does too. Some of them will definitely be getting hung on the walls of the house!

It's time for the kids to open their gifts and we call them over from playing so they can sit in the shaded area by the pond. Keegan sits behind Lyric to help her out while I help Tyler. It's amazing to see the excitement on their little faces as they open every new thing. Sometimes they'd rather play with the boxes, but we set them aside and move on to the next present.

"Before we all go back to swimmin' and playin' games, Keegan and I have one more announcement to make," I tell everyone after the last gift is opened.

"We're gonna have another baby," she tells everyone.

For a minute there's stunned silence. I'm sure they weren't expecting to hear that we were adding to our tribe so soon after the twins were born. We couldn't be happier though. Kasey is so excited and already planning the next nursery. She's got plans for a girl or a boy. I'm sure we'll implement some of them, but we'll figure that out when we get to that point.

The club did vote to buy the two houses I wasn't sure about. We decided that we would get more information about working with animals for disabled children and those would be the houses used for that. The women are ecstatic about being able to help in that way. They've even said they'll take any, and all, classes that may be needed to help the most.

Looking around the pond, I take in what has become my life. I have an amazing woman by my side. She's the rock that holds our family together, the calm to my storm, and the light to my dark. Our children are learning and growing so fast. I want to capture each and every moment with them. Before we know it, they're going to be grown and out on their own. The rest of my family is growing and becoming closer daily. We're growing the club and finding new ways to help people all the time.

Epilogue Two

Pops

I LOST THE LOVE OF MY LIFE almost two years ago. Not a day goes by that I don't miss her. If I know my Ma though, she wouldn't want me to be miserable and spend the rest of my life missing her and what we could've had together with all the new additions to our family.

I've been spending time with Alice, and she understands that I'm not ready for anything more than a friendship right now. One day I'll be ready to move us past the friendship phase of our relationship though. Alice is amazing. She listens to me when I need to talk, we go out to eat and watch movies, she's become a part of my club life, and everyone loves her. Honestly, she makes it hard not to care about her more than I already do.

Today, we're taking the kids to the pond to spend the day with them. A few of the kids have been talking about Ma, and others that we've lost along the way. So, Alice and I are going to talk about Ma and the life she led. I'm sure it's going to be hard for Alice to hear about my wife, but maybe she'll understand why I still love her so much.

"Pops?" Jameson asks me as I set down the cooler I was carrying.

"Yeah son?"

"Are we talking about Ma today. I want to know about her."

"We are. Why don't you guys sit down, and I'll hand out the sandwiches Miss Alice made before I start."

All of the kids sit down while Alice helps me get everything else set up. There are sandwiches, chips, juice boxes, and cookies for dessert. As soon as all the kids have their lunch in front of them, I sit down and pull Alice down next to me.

"I met Ma a long time ago at a pool. She was the most beautiful girl I had ever laid eyes on. That's not what made me want to get to know her though," I begin. "One day we were at the pool and an older lady was havin' trouble settin' her chair and stuff up. Instead of pickin' on her and pointin' fingers like her friends were doin', Ma walked over and helped her get everythin' set up. Then, she didn't just walk back to her friends, she sat down next to this lady and talked to her. I swear, Ma sat there for hours just listenin' to this lady talk. Several times I looked at this lady's face and could see the pure joy radiatin' off her. All she wanted was someone to talk to. Ma gave her that. It wasn't just that day though. Every single day that lady showed up at the pool, Ma would sit with her."

I go on to tell the kids about finally getting Ma to go out with me. Our first date was a disaster because I was so nervous, and I didn't think she'd ever give me a second chance. At the end of the date, she leaned over and kissed me on the cheek. It was the best ending to a date I've ever had in my life.

Jameson starts asking about how she was when his dad and aunt Bailey were growing up. So, I tell them funny stories about her playing pranks on the kids and the pranks they would play back. There was always some prank war going on in our house and sometimes I was afraid to walk in the door. I can see Jameson's eyes light up and I know that Joker, Sky, and Cage are in for a world of trouble now.

We spend the entire day talking about Ma, playing in the pond, running around, and just having fun. Today was a day that was needed by all of us. I'm glad that Alice was a part of it too. It shows that she's more like Ma than I thought.

I'm never going to replace my wife, but I will build a new life with Alice. She's been hurt and broken too. We've both got pasts and together we'll overcome all the heartache and pain we've both suffered through. Alice is patient, kind, caring, and I can feel myself falling in love with her. It may not be the same kind of love I shared with Ma, but it's love none-the-less.

Alice

Since I've had Whitney working for me, and have been able to take more time off, I have been spending more time with Pops and other members of the club. I love spending time with the kids and getting to know all of them. They're personalities are shining through and you can see how strong every single one of these kids are already.

Pops and I have spent time laughing, talking, going out to do things, and just getting to know one another. He has included me in every aspect of his life, but we're still not ready to move on past getting to know one another. We've been through this song and dance before and there's no need to rush anything now. The only difference is that he's got kids and such a large extended family, and I have none. There were never any kids for me, my family is already all gone, and my husband was killed a very long time ago.

I'm surprised that Pops wanted to include me today. This is his special time with all the kids to relieve their time with Ma and to get to know her better than they already do. I'm not sure if he wants me there as support, or if he just wants to spend time with me. Either way, I'll be there for him and the kids whenever they need me to be there for them.

As he talks about the woman that has owned his heart for most of his life, I don't get jealous of their time together. Ma helped mold this man into the person that he is today. Pops is generous, caring, would help anyone in need, and wants to be surrounded by his family. I don't know that he would be like that if it weren't for the love he shared with Ma. So, hearing about how they met and the amazing person that she was helps me understand Pops in a way. It also lets me know why Bailey does some of the things that she does. She has taken over for her mother, and it truly is a gift to be able to witness the hold this woman has over so many people still to this day.

I can honestly see myself and Pops spending what time we have left together. There's no fighting over petty things because we've already been through most everything that a person can go through. All we want to do is spend time together and be there to lend support to one another. Will we grow to love one another? Possibly. I know I care deeply about Pops. I'm just not sure about how he feels, or what he wants from us. We'll just take it a day at a time and see where it goes. As long as I get to be a part of his life, I'm good with it.

The End

Rage's Redemption Playlist

Christina Perri – Jar Of Hearts

Machine Gun Kelly – Let You Go

Rhianna – Stay

Sam Smith - Too Good At Goodbyes

Jason Aldean – Dirt Road Anthem

Jason Aldean – First Time

Lee Brice – That Don't Sound Like You

Brantley Gilbert – The Best Of Me

Brantley Gilbert – Picture On The Dashboard

DMX – Ruff Ryders' Anthem

2Pac – Dear Mama

Cole Swindell – Making My Way To You

Cole Swindell – I Just Want You

Acknowledgements

First and foremost, I have to thank my team. Darlene, Jenni, and my new PA Michelle. You have kept me on track, talked through holes in the story, and just been there for me. I don't know that this book would've made it if it weren't for you all. I love you guys!

My beta team is amazing! You have talked me down from being nervous about this book and let me know your honest opinion of the story. If there's problems with the book, you let me know so I can put out a good story for the readers. Thank you for everything!

Graphics by Shelly as always has given me an amazing cover for this story. I love all of the teasers, covers, and other graphics that you have done for me. Thank you so much for making sure that I love the final product and taking time to make sure that everything is there and correct!!

My family has been a tremendous support system to me. You give me time to write, do my takeovers, and whatever else I need to do in order to continue to put these stories out there. I love you all to the moon and back!

The readers that follow me, and show me unwavering support. Without you this wouldn't be possible. I will never be able to thank you enough for all the support and love of my books that you have shown me since I started this journey. I promise that I will be attending signings soon so that I can meet some of you!! Thank you just doesn't seem enough to show you how much you truly mean to me.

About The Author

I am a single mom of three amazing children, living in Upstate New York. We have lived in New York forever and I can't wait to start showing my kids other states.

I developed a love for reading at a young age from my grandma. My kids are following in my footsteps and read almost as much as I do. I read anything I can get my hands on. Now, I get to live my dream and put my own stories out in the world.

If I'm not writing, or reading, you can find me hanging out with my kids, watching NASCAR, and teaching my kids how to bake. We love to bake and learn how to make new things. I also love to rearrange my house every so often. It tends to drive some people around me crazy!

One fact about me is that I'm extremely shy. I love meeting new people and hearing stories about their lives. You can meet so many amazing and interesting people by just taking a few minutes to listen!

Here are some links to follow me:

Facebook:
https://www.facebook.com/ErinOsborneAuthor/
Twitter:
https://twitter.com/author_osborne
My website:
http://erinosborne1013.wix.com/authorerinosborne
Spotify:
https://open.spotify.com/user/emgriff07

Note to the Readers

First, I would like to thank you all for taking a chance on me when I released Skylar's Saviors. With every book I release, I have a million questions running through my head. It doesn't get any easier the more books you release.

Rage's Redemption is the last book in the Clifton Falls Wild Kings MC series. This book has me more nervous than any of the other ones. I'm not sure if it's because it's the last book or not. This series has taken me on a wild ride and most things even surprised me as I was writing the story.

I have to thank you all for the amazing show of support you have shown me over the last year especially. I have had several life changing events occur in the last few months and have had to take some time off writing and interacting with you all. You all have shown nothing but support and love as I've taken care of my personal problems and been there when I've started writing again. So many of you have shown so much love and what the Indie community is truly about. We should always show love and support to one another. If you ever need to talk or someone to just be in your corner, feel free to PM me.

I look forward to seeing what the next series has in store for us all. Thank you for the continued support and love!